SIN CITY WRITERS GROUP ANTHOLOGY VOLUME ONE

MORE SELECTIONS FROM BLUEBERRY LANE BOOKS

Anthologies

DRASTIC MEASURES (Vol. 1)

WASH THE SPIDER OUT (DM Vol. 2)

UNIVERSAL ENIGMA (DM Vol. 3)

Books by

Michele M. Green

THE ISLAND RAN RED

THE ISLAND BRUISED BLUE

THE ISLAND SOLD OUT

THE ISLAND STOOD STILL

Irving A. Greenfield

ANCIENT OF DAYS

WHARF SINISTER

MASS FOR A DEAD WITCH

ONLY THE DEAD SPEAK RUSSIAN

A PLAY OF DARKNESS

SNOW GIANTS DANCING

BEYOND VALOR

Ben Parris

WADE OF AQUITAINE

KREINDIA OF AMORIUM

AMYNTA OF ANATOLIA

MARS ARMOR FORGED

CREDS: THE IRS ADVENTURE

TODAY YOU WRITE THE BOOK

Ben Parris and William Friedman

SUPERNATURALZ WEIRD CREEPY & RANDOM

Jim Hohenbary

BEFORE THE RUINS

SIN CITY WRITERS GROUP ANTHOLOGY VOLUME ONE

Edited by Ben Parris and H.G. McKinnis

SIN CITY WRITERS GROUP ANTHOLOGY
Volume 1

FIRST U.S. EDITION

Cover photo by Ben Parris
Cover art by Kevin Michaels
Cover models (by permission): Lucy Couch and Ian Sweet Couch
Silas (the cat) photos courtesy of Linda Jones Weber

Library of Congress Cataloging In-Publication Data
has been applied for

ISBN 978-1-942183-21-1
www.Blueberrylanebooks.com

For Toni

"She was unlike any writer I have ever known. I can still remember the first time I heard her read a piece of her work. Her voice, her words, the way the whole room went quiet—it left an indelible mark on me. But as much as I loved her writing, it was Toni as a person who truly touched my life. I will forever admire her tenacity and heart."

~Amanda Skenandore

CONTENTS

Toni K. Pacini
Author of *Alabama Blue:*
A Southern Gothic Memoir
Founder, Sin City Writers Group
7/18/54 - 10/25/24

When Last We Saw Toni

There's never a Tuesday I don't think of Toni. That's the day I leap into the writing critique fray at Skinny Dugans Casino and Lounge. Not only was this Toni's chosen place, but also the drive takes me past the home of Amanda Skenendore, the best friend and former nurse who took Toni in and cared for her in her final battle with metastatic cancer.

As I write this message, I sit reading an amazing book from Toni's personal collection, *An Original Sin*, an S.G. Tasz *Dead Mall* novella. The inscription reads, in part, "...you will probably want to start with this." I picture Toni sitting and devouring them all with great pleasure, as I know she did. Tasz is the Sin City Writers Group member to whom Toni passed the torch, along with a whole team of moderators.

In the fall of 2024, H.G. McKinnis and I went to see Toni at her bedside knowing she would want us to read to her from our current work. If we could provide Toni with one extra ounce of service or comfort, we were going to do it. Not wanting to be left out, her amazing gigantic Maine Coon, Silas, joined us, brushing past our legs like a slinking jungle cat and then climbing the oversized cat tree to the highest perch.

When we entered her room, Toni sat right up to plant a kiss on my cheek. What struck me most about her was how quickly she could spot a kindred soul and make an instant connection. H.G. and I only knew Toni for one out of seventy years, from October to October, but what a triumphant period it was, filled with the adoration of her longtime friends and fellow writers, including a large gathering for her birthday that year. Well into her battle with cancer, the get-together served as tribute and farewell, a send-off filled with testimonials about how she changed her friends' lives.

With a small core group, Toni had created a weekly meeting for Sin City Writers in 2016, which was later expanded to two days to meet the demand. In our visit, we talked about the future of the group. She agreed that it needed a Henderson location and another day of the week.

We didn't know how close to the end she was. The very next day, Saturday, October 20, 2024, she would astound everyone by venturing out to the Las Vegas Book Festival in 2024 at the Historic Fifth Street School in downtown Las Vegas. I think she wanted to see their featured guest, John Waters.

I have a habit of carrying my latest work-in-progress and sitting down to make changes wherever I go, alternating between fresh printouts of my latest work and handwritten mark-up between the printout's double-spaced lines. This includes replaced words and new passages. When we went to visit Toni I had my 2024 Halloween contest story, my only copy with the edits.

H.G. read hers to Toni's delight and I read mine. H.G. and I tend to build some comedy into our work. Then Toni asked to see it up close. Perusing the first page of my notes, laughing, lips moving, she stopped and said, "I'm keeping this."

Gathering my papers to her chest, she crossed her arms over them with a smile on her face and went to sleep.

Ben Parris,
February, 2026
Henderson, Nevada

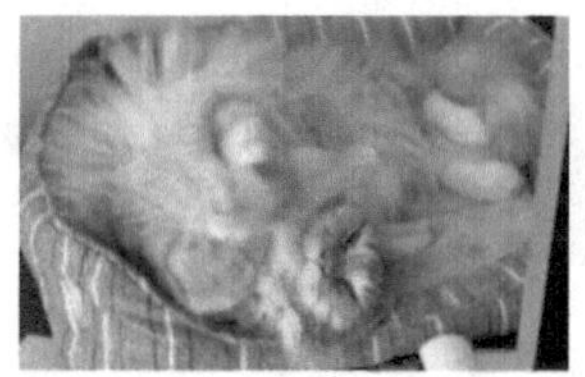

Sin City Writers Group Anthology
Volume 1

The first modern "crit" sessions took place in the salons of Europe and "mutual improvement" clubs of America beginning in the 17th century with such luminaries as Jean Baptiste Molière, and later, Charles Dickens and Benjamin Franklin. The first half of the 20th century saw the formation of The Bloomsbury Group with London's Virginia Woolf and E.M. Forster, the Algonquin Group featuring New York City's Dorothy Parker and Robert Benchley, and The Inklings that included J.R.R. Tolkien and C.S. Lewis. It's hard to imagine the level of discourse that flowed from these electric combinations. All I can summon to mind is the coffee shop banter of the Beat Generation, having met a few of the survivors.

But our greatest inspiration was the collaboration described to us by Ray Bradbury, George Clayton Johnson, and William F. Nolan, who provided firsthand information on a magical combination generically known as the West Coast Writers Group. Under Charles Beaumont (who wrote 22 episodes of *The Twilight Zone*) in the 1950s and 1960s, the group was aptly known as the Southern California Sorcerers because of their productivity and penchant for science fiction and the supernatural. Rod Serling's memorial foundation tells us that at its peak, this association of creative artists also included Rod Serling, Richard Matheson, Robert Bloch, Jerry Sohl, Ray Russell, and Harlan Ellison, among others. Their friendships extended to professional relationships where members helped foster the careers of one another.

Of course, that phenomenon grew out of Hollywood and the networks operating in the show biz center of gravity, pulling together the greatest of talents in the early days.

Fast forward to twenty first century New York, the long-time mecca of publishing where I grew up, and you have every type of writer's group with curiously modest results.

On the crowded end of the spectrum, I once joined a group of 250 active members in an auditorium where a man fought for the microphone only to share that he had seen a rat in the parking lot. In a Barnes & Noble meetup we had the more civil circle of 30. Best of all was a group of four to six active Long Island writers who produced more than twenty-five novels.

We see Sin City Writers Group, just reaching its first decade with an average of 15 active participants per session with dozens of books written, providing brilliant critiques as the closest thing we have today showing the potential to reach the level of the amazing talent pool and camaraderie seen in Beaumont's group.

In the first section of our Sin City Writer's Group Anthology Volume One, the reader will find the results of a contest inspired by our country's 250th anniversary coinciding with SCWG's 10th anniversary in 2026. The second section is a showcase of our membership's talents with genres ranging from science fiction to romance, made up of short stories and book excerpts.

Ben Parris and H.G. McKinnis for

Blueberry Lane Books
Henderson, Nevada,
February, 2026

Part I: Flag Contest

In honor of our nation's 250th birthday—a moment that also marks the 10th anniversary of Sin City Writers Group—we hosted a short story writing contest open to all members. This event invited participants to reflect on and creatively interpret this historic milestone, celebrating both our country's enduring legacy and a decade of shared creativity within our group. Here we proudly present the winners.

First place: Chris Battle

Second Place: Zoran Sova

Third Place: Chris Valdez

Honorable Mention: E.J. Siegler

George Washington's Teeth

Chris Battle

I was in the copy room when our Museum Registrar, Mz. Fernheart approached.

"Mr. Goodbottom. Please escort George Washington's teeth to the National Restoration Lab, then return.

I nodded. "Well, ok."

"Sign here."

I complied.

"She handed me one white glove and placed a small, wooden carrier in my arms like a baby that happened to be the Father of His Country. "Don't let them rattle." She turned and left.

I googled the legality of taking a Founding Father's molars on public transportation. The AI that lived in my phone was uncertain. Then I researched the teeth. They weren't his alone. Nor were they made of wood. Apparently, George Washington had a small nation inside his mouth; his and other people's teeth, basting in yummy eighteenth-century adhesives.

I felt patriotic. Then, ridiculous for feeling patriotic about a bite set. Then I felt patriotic again because the pendulum of American feeling is complicated.

AT THE DC METRO station, the wind followed the train and sent the case vibrating like a drum in a rock band. I angled the box against my rib cage, forming a fleshy wrap.

I hopped onboard. The train started then stopped. A speaker broadcast: *We're holding for "protest activity" outside.*

A young man sitting across from me glared at my wooden carrier. "You got something valuable there?" he asked.

"I do," I responded, immediately sorry.

"Want help?" he said, grabbing the handle unbidden.

"No thank you." I tightened my grip like American independence.

The train jerked forward. He tugged, trying to free the case from my grip.

"You don't understand," I said. Then, I popped the latch with my thumb, slipped my gloved hand inside, and showed him the teeth.

They were neither shining nor monstrous. Simply present in a way that made you proud. For a second, the young man's expression achieved something like reverence. Then confusion.

"Yeow!" he shouted. "What are those?"

"George Washington's teeth," I said. "Composite."

He let go immediately.

He must have realized he had, in broad daylight,

attempted to abscond with the nation's mandible celebrity. A small circle of people noticed. An older man tipped his cap and bowed.

The young man evaporated into the crowd.

I re-latched the case and resumed breathing.

Standing to offer an elderly woman my seat, I set the case on the ground. When I next looked - the case was gone!

My panic became shock. No sweating, just surveying. Seat: empty. Floor: gum and a faded penny.

The Registrar's last words echoed: *Don't let them rattle.* They were rattling somewhere else entirely now.

I dialed the museum and was put on hold. A piccolo version of the national anthem played. From watching TV crime shows, I knew how precious the minutes after an abduction were. I hung up.

Then I did what any citizen would if they had misplaced a national artifact. I searched social media.

I typed "wooden carrier, antique mystery box inside. Metro," then "found teeth" into my phone. I got a quick response.

On a channel designed to highlight the day's oddities, a thumbnail sketch appeared. A young man's light-ring-lit face, ecstatic with discovery. The banner beneath: OMG FOUND THIS INSANE BOX ON THE METRO #MysteryBox #Unboxing.

I tapped. A teenage boy beamed into his phone. Behind him, the wooden case sat open on a table. "Hey, patriots, Master again," he said, and winked. "Today we got, like, a literal historic vibe. Someone left this on the train. Smash that *like* if interested."

Comments bloomed like red algae.

Open it.

Do it!

He released the latch, slowly, for suspense. There were the teeth, reclining in velvet. Not grotesque, simply there with the intense dignity of historic objects. He leaned close. "I think it's…dentures?" He looked delighted. "This is so metal."

The chat erupted.

Ewwww, wood?

Like. #GeorgeChompington.

So gross.

The kid read the card the museum keeps with objects: chain-of-custody number, collection, destination. He sounded it out. "National…Res-tor-ation Lab." He looked up at the camera with holy mischief. "Should we call them?"

"YES," I said to my phone, then realized yelling was not contact.

I messaged the account name. "Hi!" I typed, and deleted, because enthusiasm can look suspicious. Redo. "Hello. I'm with the Museum. You found an item of ours. We can pick it up."

He didn't reply. Busy reading comments like a DJ taking requests.

New tactic. "Brand partnership opportunity." It hurt my heart to type those words. Thief. "Would you be open to a collab with the Museum? Quick call?"

My phone flashed: *Seen.*

Then: *omg hi. collab how*. A sunglass emoji.

I said, "We'd love to feature content about stewardship of artifacts." I suppressed the thought of our lead conservator's head bursting into flames.

Lol what is stewardship, he wrote.

"Caring for things that outlast us," I typed. "Also: we need the item back, today!"

He replied with a voice memo. He sounded softer than the video. *"Okay, brand person,"* he said. *"I live like two stops from the Mall. Come up. But let's do a video together? History is so dead, you know? Let's make it live."*

I sent a thumbs-up and asked for his address. When it came, I acted. Not seeking permission.

THE BUILDING WAS NEW. I buzzed.

In person, he was smaller. His place had the curated mess of someone whose living room was a film set.

My teeth sat on a lazy Susan, spinning slowly, illuminated.

"Hey," he said, introducing me to his audience. "This is the museum brand person. We're doing a stewardship collab."

"I'm just an intern," I said.

He laughed as if I'd made a joke about the human condition. "Same," he said, and spun the teeth gently. "Dude. These are, like, the OG veneers."

"They're a composite," I said, because apparently that's how I'm wired. "Human teeth, ivory, metal, springs. Nothing wooden. That's a myth."

He nodded, appreciative. "Busted," he told his camera. "No wood in the wood teeth. History is lies." He tilted the phone. "What's your name?"

My brain spun. Providing my name felt like a liability.

"I represent Collections. We need to get those to the Restoration Lab today.

He sat on the edge of the sofa. "I want to do the right thing, but I also want people to see this. Like, we never *see* the stuff. It's always glass between. This is *real*, and here. And kind of gross in a beautiful way, and that's America."

"The counter-argument is that being seen destroys things."

"I get it," he said, surprisingly. "What if we do both? You take them. But I film you walking down the hall carrying the box. Anonymous. You're, like, the guardian of teeth. Hashtag #Stewardship. I'll say: we touched history, and now we put it back."

It was elegant, in the way of eighteen-year-olds discovering nobility.

"I need to verify you haven't damaged them," I said. "But we can't show the interior on camera."

He nodded. "Oops. We did, like, a little open," he said. "But I didn't touch. I used my ring light, though. Is that bad?"

"Light is a concept we manage," I said, which is museum for "yes."

"May I?" I asked, putting on my glove. He got quiet. I checked the clasps, the supports, the brittle places. Nothing looked different.

He watched me the way people watch competence when they're deciding if they can love it. "You really care about this," he said, as a question.

"I'm being graded," I said, and then, because honesty arrives at odd times, "Also, yes."

We filmed a single take, down the hall to the elevator. He

narrated in a church-like whisper. "Sometimes you find something and you think it's yours," he said, "But it's not. It's ours in a different way. Stewardship means we get to *have* it by letting someone else *keep* it. Smash that *like* for responsibility!"

At the elevator he said: "Don't let them rattle."

Surprised, I answered "I won't."

AT THE LAB, the conservator listened with a trace of a smile. How I located the teeth via a livestream and retrieved them via diplomacy.

"I checked them. They look fine," she said. "You got them back by telling someone they mattered." Her tone suggested I had done something right, and I looked down so I wouldn't enjoy it too much.

BACK AT THE MUSEUM, I stood in the Registrar's doorway. Mz. Fernheart asked, "Did the transfer occur?"

I said yes.

She said, "Any incidents?"

"I briefly lost visual contact on public transportation," I admitted.

"Duration?"

"Under three hours," I replied.

"Any rattling?"

"None," I said, feeling the high and low of a beautifully executed lie.

"Oh, she said, swiveling her computer monitor so I could

see it. I received a request from a producer of a popular history podcast re your recent 'intern collaboration' today. Asking you to speak on *stewardship*. Interested?"

She knows everything. "Uh, sure."

"Good. I'll answer yes," she said, typing. "And congratulations on your promotion! Oh look."

I stared at her monitor. A thousand little red hearts floated up the screen in agreement.

Chris Battle calls herself a word sculptor. Her husband calls her "Hey you." It works out.

Chicago born, after acting as fourth dancing princess from the left in Sleeping Beauty, at Jane Adams- Hull House, she's been dancing, acting and writing ever since.

Chris has lived in New York City, Tampa, Florida, and finally Las Vegas with her husband and family. She's interacted with the creative communities everywhere they lived, still in touch with some online.

In Vegas, she belongs to the Sin City Writers Group, The Henderson Writers Group, and recently cofounded a playwrights group called PlaywrightsStagewerksLV.

Small American Flag

Zoran Sova

"I'm an American, they won't hurt me!" Mark, a young man with a close-cropped haircut, shouted over the hiss of bullets. We lay behind a row of jagged boulders – our last cover. Death crawled down the rugged terrain of the mountain slope, carried by twenty Bosnian soldiers and their mujahedeen allies. They slipped from rock to rock, closing the hundred-yard gap, and soon the flames of their hatred would engulf us.

I turned to Mark. "You're welcome to surrender, my American friend." When he realized that the four of us had no intention of doing so, disbelief twisted his face. "You don't stand a chance; you'll die in vain."

From our left side, Ivan crawled over to us. His helmet gone, the sunlight glinted off the scar carved into his face. Barely twenty, and far too young to comprehend the gravity of what we faced.

"The moment we signed up for the army, death became our constant companion," he said.

The sun had baked us all day and refused to sink behind

the mountain peaks, not allowing night to give us a chance to escape.

"Marina!" I called. "How is it up there!?"

She turned, her uniform torn by shrapnel, her long brown hair tied in a dusty ponytail. Fear etched itself onto her round face, her lips pressed tight, jaw clenched as if biting down on the last thread of life.

"We're surrounded." She nodded toward the meadow behind us. "Can we make a run for it?"

I didn't look back. The meadow cut between the rugged mountain ridges, luring us with the dark woods at its ends. It looked like our only hope.

"Mines." I said flatly. "The whole field is mined."

From the right, Ante rolled toward us. The left arm of his uniform was soaked in dark red. We'd wrapped his shoulder earlier, but the fabric was saturated with blood.

"Better to die on a mine than wait for the butchers," he said firmly. The oldest in the group, only halfway to thirty, and silver threads had already begun to weave through his dark hair.

"What do you think, Mark?" I asked the American.

WE'D FOUND HIM by accident, patrolling the western side of the high mountain. He'd been sitting by a dirt road, tired and thirsty from a long walk. We watched him from the forest shadows before stepping out. As soon as he saw us, he jumped to his feet and raised a small flag. He didn't even reach for his rifle. United Nations Protection Force (UNPROFOR) soldiers hadn't come to fight, but to protect civilians and organize humanitarian help.

"I'm an American!" he shouted.

We approached cautiously and checked his documents.

"Where are you going?" I asked. *How had he ended up here alone*?

"I got lost." He glanced around nervously, which I understood. He probably had no idea which army we belonged to, or what to expect from us. His gaze flicked over my shoulder, searching for a military insignia.

"Don't worry." I offered him a soft smile. "We are friendly. Did you call your command for help?"

"They told me to head to Jablanica."

"Jablanica?" Marina cut in. "It's pronounced Yablanitza."

"Yes, exactly!" he replied eagerly. "Can you tell me which way?"

"You're on the right path," I said, pointing east. "The town is on the other side of the mountain. You can make it before dark …"

A short burst of gunfire from the direction of the forest cut me off. Ante ran up to us. "The Muslims are coming," he said. "We have to move!" Blood dripped down his left sleeve.

"Are you hurt?" I asked.

"Nothing serious."

No time to talk. The only way out was down a bare slope, where we would be exposed to enemy fire.

"Call for help," I told the American.

At first confused, he managed to get a distress call out, before the whizzing of bullets forced us to run downhill. We'd stop now and then, hiding behind large rocks to fire back in short, sharp bursts.

AND THAT'S HOW we ended up in this hopeless situation. In front of us local Muslims and foreign mujahideen, behind us a minefield. My canteen gave me the last drops of water, and I tossed it empty into the grass. I wouldn't need it anymore; dawn would never come for me.

"Here's what we'll do," I said. "I'll stay behind to cover the retreat. You guys are going to cross the minefield."

"This is madness!" shouted Mark, lost in a land he couldn't find on a globe.

Right then, it felt like even God had forgotten us. *Jesus, how to ask this question*? "I need a volunteer to go first."

"I'll go," said both Ante and Ivan.

Shit. I had to choose who would be the first to step on a mine. I hesitated, my thoughts buzzing like a swarm of bees.

"Ante goes first," I decided. "Then Ivan, Marina, and the American. Keep a distance ten meters apart." I figured that Marina and the American had a chance to survive.

He stared at me. "You're sending your soldiers to certain death." I met his gentle eyes, full of the colors of spring, and I was sure that they had never seen

human monstrosity.

"We call it a Death relay." Sour smile ~~on~~ as my face tried and failed to justify my decision. "As your Lakota chief Crazy Horse said, it's a good day to die."

Suddenly, a helicopter appeared in the distance, slicing through the sky from the direction of the mountain peak. Hope raised its head, and the American jumped, as if bitten by a snake, and began waving his arms. He exposed himself to bloodthirsty eyes searching for a target. It was all in vain;

the helicopter roared overhead, passing us by without so much as noticing us.

"It will come back around!" he shouted to me. "We just need to get their attention!" He pulled an American flag from his backpack, but it was small, and I doubted the pilot could spot it. Then it hit me—I called out to my group: "Give me your flags!"

They quickly handed their Croatian flags over. On each side of the American flag, I tied one of ours. That gave us a large, colorful banner. I looked up at the blue sky. The helicopter was returning, still too high.

"Guys, give us cover!" I ordered, and then turned to the American.

"It's time to dance."

We raised the flags as high as our arms could reach and waved them. A rain of bullets showered us, but we didn't stop. The sky exploded with the thunder of the helicopter, then it was gone in a heartbeat. We hurled ourselves behind the rocks.

"Do you think they saw us?" Mark asked.

The day was dimming before my eyes; I could barely see him. *Was the sun finally setting, or were my eyes failing?*

"Damn it, Petar, you're bleeding!" He crawled over to me. "Guys, Petar is wounded!"

Marina tossed a magazine to Ivan and rushed to me. She ripped open my shirt and revealed a nasty wound on my right side, somewhere below the lungs. Working fast, she pulled a bandage from her bag, took off her shirt, pressed it to the bloody wound, and wrapped it. Next moment I was slapped.

"Don't fall asleep!" she yelled.

I grinned. "Don't worry, girl, I promised to be your baby's godfather."

Marina didn't have a child—she wasn't even married yet—but we had made promises to each other about what we'd do after the war. That kept us going in moments of despair. The shooting intensified; they were coming to finish us off before dark. We could no longer even make it into the minefield.

"Go help Ante and Ivan," I ordered Marina.

Her face wore a farewell glance.

I raised my left hand and pointed Mark to a smaller rock further downhill. "Hide there, and when they come, tell them you're American. Maybe they'll spare you."

He turned me toward the enemy and shoved a rifle in my hands. "Goodbye, brother." He spat to the side and climbed toward the others. The Dire Straits song *Brothers in Arms* ran through my head.

Though the wound was bandaged, the blood—and with it my life—was slowly draining. Surprisingly, I didn't feel fear. Maybe it had drained away with the blood. The thought made me laugh. I should smile now—let them see I died happy. Everything blurred in my mind—gunfire, explosions, screams. The cacophony of sounds faded, and darkness closed in.

WHITE LIGHT SEARED my eyes. *Was heaven too bright*? Then, through the white mist, a face emerged. Then another, and another. I recognized my soldiers. Sitting on chairs by my hospital bed. All of them alive. And among them—the

American.

"What are you doing here?" I managed to ask on the third try.

"I brought a gift for you!" he exclaimed. From his bag, he pulled out a brand-new American flag and gently placed it on the pillow beside me.

"I hope we meet again in the U.S. soon," he said, a smile lighting up his face.

Zoran Sova was born in 1962 in the former Yugoslavia. He graduated from University of Sarajevo and immigrated to Las Vegas in 2001, where he has lived since. He published a book of poetry, "Spread your Wings" in Croatia in 2000. Vanori contributed to *Trip Sheet Magazine* from 2005-2010 with a series of articles titled "To be or not to be Taxi driver." Zoran also published a short story collection titled "Difficult Decisions." He published four books for kids in Croatia:

Famous Hunters

World of Imaginations

Luka's adventures, and

Princesses

His first Book in English is *Little Dragon*.

Honoring the Flag

Chris Valdez

The crowd shouted and chanted furious words. Tolerance at an end, they demanded change. Under the dim light of the setting sun, the smoke from the flickering flames cast a disapproving shadow that few discerning eyes could see.

"Disgraceful," whispered the wind through the shadow. "Desecration."

A second whispering shadow responded, "Oh, come now, John. They're angry."

"I recognize that they're angry, Franklin. I approve of anger. Rage is what moves society to change. But what is to be the nature of that change? For the better or for the worse? This gesture speaks quite clearly for the worst."

"It's a scrap of cloth, Mr. Adams," said a new wisp of vapor. "Fabric and dye."

"It is a flag, Jefferson. A flag. And not just any flag. It is the banner of freedom for our United States. We fought and struggled for that freedom. I do not wish to see these angry people throw away that which we purchased with blood."

The shade of Benjamin Franklin grew stern. "That freedom

of which you boast includes the right to burn the flag, John."

"Mr. Adams," Jefferson added, "Remember that we both advocated for the Bill of Rights. We made suggestions. Those included the right of protest. These people are simply exercising the rights we determined to guarantee them."

"Protest is healthy and necessary," Adams argued. "But there should be exceptions for the symbols of our republic. The American flag should be regarded as holy and sacrosanct."

"Patriotism is not a religion, Mr. Adams. The nation is not a god that can command obedience. She must continue to earn the people's loyalty and respect. If she fails in that regard, then the people have the right and even the duty to demonstrate their displeasure."

Franklin added his wisdom. "That object they are burning is not the true flag, John. The United States flag is not a physical thing. It is something branded on the American soul. And this fire cannot destroy it. But weakening the freedoms it stands for might do so."

"It is my opinion-," Adams started.

"Yes, John. We have heard your opinions. You have never held back on expressing them. But perhaps, just this once, you might try listening rather than speaking. Try it for the novelty of the experience."

"And what should I be listening to, Franklin?"

"Why, to me, of course. I am the wisest person you know."

"See that, Jefferson? And he accuses me of being too fond of my own opinions."

"Mr. Adams, perhaps all three of us suffer from that malady. But let us hear Dr. Franklin out," Jefferson suggested.

"Fine. Franklin, you have the floor. Astound us."

"Thank you very much. It seems to me that the American character is a perfect example of Plato's Allegory, constantly moving from ignorance to enlightenment. You certainly recall the seventh president of these states. His actions were clearly illegal and violated our Constitution. Yet the nation survived."

"It nearly did not," Adams remarked.

"My point, sir. My very point. We were stronger on the other side of him."

"The republic must be tested periodically," Jefferson explained. "She responds to each crisis and develops a greater strength."

"Am I not supposed to be listening to Franklin?" Adams said. "Your voice seems unnecessary here."

"When I am agreeing with the points Dr. Franklin is making, then I am granted the privilege of speaking in support. And I say he is right about the strength we gained after the abuses of that particular president. We grow in strength after every crisis."

"Thank you, Tom," Franklin said. "And that truth was even truer of the war over slavery. John, surely you remember that Tom here included a condemnation of the practice in his original draft of the Declaration. A fine work, Tom. A treasure. It is truly a shame that the nation was not ready for our ideals."

"We were proven right, I think, in the end," Jefferson commented. "These people would be free."

Unable to stay silent, Adams weighed in. "My cousin predicted the conflict, Franklin. While we dithered in the

Congress over whether our new nation would continue to permit slavery, Sam Adams wrote to you that there would be trouble within a century should we surrender on the slavery issue and that posterity would never forgive us. The result was violence and destruction. Yet history has mocked us as slave-owners who demanded freedom."

"We don't matter, John. The glory of Adams, Jefferson, and Franklin was never our goal. We succeeded in our original task and have been slowly claiming new victories ever since. That conflict between the states was predictable and regrettable and based on the crime against nature that was American slavery. But you were right. And Sam was right. And Tom was right. America rejected that sinful practice. As we knew it would, eventually. We have grown."

"Are we still growing? Where do we go now?" Adams asked. "Americans despising Americans. Our nation is tearing itself apart. Do you see a path forward?"

"The future, Mr. Adams, seldom shows its cards," Jefferson reminded him. "Do remember that England and France went through their own crises of identity. And like our own internal conflict, they weathered the storm, growing stronger through the ideals they forged. These United States can surely do the same."

"Not this way. They are burning the flag. They are showing contempt for the nation itself. What unifies them without that flag? The nation's glorious spark has fizzled away to nothing. And they do this on July 4th. The anniversary of mine and Jefferson's deaths. Is this how we are to be remembered?"

"John, you should have taken to the stage," Franklin said.

"Your talent for drama and theatrics is so much greater than your skill at diplomacy."

"Diplomacy has no more use. The nation is at its own throat."

"Think back to before the Revolution. Recall that occasion when George invited us to dine at his house?"

"Which George?" Adams asked. "It was a common name. You couldn't toss a brick without hitting three or four Georges."

"Yes, and what a delightful pastime that was. So sad that brick-tossing has fallen into disfavour as an evening's revelry. But I was referring to Washington, of course."

"What about him? Why is he not here? Does he not care about the decline of the country he fought to create?"

Jefferson laughed. "Your voice, Mr. Adams, can be abrasively repellent. He can fret and worry anywhere he likes without subjecting himself to your noise."

"Well said," Franklin approved. "Back to the point I was making. John, you and I attended a dinner at George's house once."

"I remember. I remember."

"You happened to remark on the large Bible displayed on its own podium in the corner of the dining room. What did you say of it?"

"I said that it showed little signs of use. What good is a Bible if one does not open it up and read it from time to time? In George's house, it was nothing more than furniture."

"Precisely, John. Precisely. Very well remembered. But America has its own Bible. It is not the flag, but the Constitution. It is our duty to give obedience to those words.

America's Bible clearly protects every American's right to free speech and protest. If we start protecting the flag at the expense of our rights, what will be our next exemption? Today, it is a flag. Tomorrow, will it be a statue? Or a person? What rights will we give up as we choose a new idol? What meaning does our flag even hold if the Constitution is no longer upheld as sacred law?"

The whispers on the wind went still as the protests continued. Yelling and screaming. Signs held aloft. Children crying, disturbed by the strange and alarming sounds that had replaced tonight's bedtime.

Then Adams spoke again. "I take your point, Franklin. But is it your opinion that America should have no symbols they regard as inviolable?"

"Symbols are dangerous, John. They come to replace that which they are meant to represent. How many Christians honour the cross and ignore the words of Christ? It is the ideals of America that should take precedent, not the symbols. The flag is nothing but a reminder. If we wave the flag and abandon what it stands for, then we are lost."

"You favour this gesture then? The burning of the American flag?"

"I favour the right to do so," Franklin responded. "Arresting them for their protests and for their speech would betray the principles for which we fought."

"I concur," Jefferson agreed.

"Franklin. Jefferson. Damn you both. You've made your case. I withdraw my objection. But do not expect me to stay and watch this disrespect."

"Very good, John. We shall retire from this field. Let us

seek out a tavern and enjoy the camaraderie."

"Not tonight, Franklin. Abigail is waiting."

Chris Valdez was born and raised in New Mexico and moved to Las Vegas in the late 90s. He wrote his first story at five years old and has been hooked on the craft ever since. He has written short stories, novels, employee manuals, and a play.

The Last Word

E.J. Siegler

We almost gave up. The grey pollution-filled sky streaked with reddish-brown hues from our dying sun signaled that night was coming. That meant trouble. The darkness would make navigating our way to our campsite treacherous, and we would be easy pickings for the mutations. Some might say the mutations were the unlucky ones. The losers of the war, as if anyone in a war could be considered a winner. For the past 50 years, those of us who survived spent every day either fending off predators or scavenging for the few edible morsels of food uncontaminated by radiation.

If survivors didn't lose a limb or an organ along the way, they lost friends, lovers, and children. After the bombs fell, as my great-grandfather used to tell it, it took over two years for the air to become breathable again. For another 10 years, masks were mandatory, forcibly cleaning a small percentage of toxins so our bodies could inhale enough oxygen to survive.

What happened? In the 50 years that passed, we adapted. Like all creatures, humans found a way. Our lungs don't require as high a concentration of the 'O' as Granpappy did. What we do require is churned out by giant silver machines powered by the ever-shifting winds, bottled, and circulated in limited quantities.

Our ancestors would think it a strange world they passed on. A legacy left by a generation more concerned with personal gain than with caring for the planet that gave us life.

Today marks the anniversary of the beginning of the end as we know it. July 4, 2030. Through the miracle of technology and some assistance from our nurturing mother Gaia, who, despite being torn asunder, has slowly, impossibly, begun to heal. No, a single plant didn't sprout amongst stacks of garbage. Rather, patches of weeds and crabgrass returned to the surface. The suckers came with a vengeance, growing unchecked with spikes instead of smooth blades, but they came back, bringing hope and enough additional oxygen to end the rationing.

We still celebrate the 4th. Few people remain alive who remember what the day meant, but we've all heard the stories. Bright colored lights shot into the air to simulate bombs bursting in the air. Granpappy used to sit me on his lap as we watched the streaming reds, whites, and blues rocket against the smoke-filled sky.

"Sonny." He called everyone Sonny, even my sister. "Ironic, isn't it? We built a day to celebrate blowing up those who oppressed us, so we could oppress others. It is an endless circle. It's almost fitting that during 'Independence Day'," Granpappy's voice turned bitter, "we started the final war."

I stand now, in the center of it all. Somewhere I'm told was once called Washington, DC, the former home of the Capitol building, long buried beneath smoking rubble. The first missile struck here, then another. No one remembers who fired them. It doesn't matter. Once one exploded, all the missiles across the world were launched, each targeting a different object of hate.

My team and I are the first people to venture this close to Area Zero. I expected a crater, but it's filled by metal, marble, and cement, all fused from the nuclear heat. Huge, with a diameter of over 20 kilometers. A river once flowed here, according to the maps. Although our instruments indicate radiation levels that border on the yellow safe zone, we are protected by personal safety coverings. We've been digging all day, hoping to find something, anything, that will give us a clue to what our ancestors were thinking.

We've found nothing, of course. It was foolish to think otherwise. Nothing could have survived the vicious barrage and subsequent mushroom cloud. Even mutations avoid this area. As the streaks in the sky fade to light pink, I make the signal to shut the operation down. *We can come back tomorrow, but we won't,* I think, packing my laser shovel into its case. *There is nothing here.*

"Captain." My second in command approaches, his voice steady, concealing disappointment. He comes from a long line of soldiers, his family well-populated with generals and admirals throughout the years. His grandmother survived to pass on the legacy, and yet he still insisted on joining the closest thing to a military we have. I admire his dedication. The day he showed up in my unit comes to mind.

"Captain, Sir. Private Stantion reporting for duty."

For the first time since I formed the New Hope Army, I smiled.

"Stand down, sonny," I said, adopting my Granpappy's informal greeting. "We don't stand on formality here."

He relaxed his posture just slightly, but answered, "Yes, Sir."

Since that day, he has remained the perfect soldier, doing everything by the book, despite all the curves our world throws at him. Some of the team laughs at him, or so I'm told. They don't do it when I'm around. I've grown to appreciate his dedication to a past that gave up on people like him long ago.

"At ease, Lieutenant." If I didn't say it, he would never drop his hand from his forehead.

"Captain, you should come here, we found something."

I shrugged. Most likely, nothing more than a piece of a missile or a shell casing. Still, those would be a welcome addition to our museum. I decide to humor him.

"Lead on, Lieutenant."

We walk about 100 paces toward the setting sun to one of the first holes dug today. The lung-clogging dust we raised has settled down, making it easier to see what lies below. With the lieutenant's help, I ease my way down the slippery slope until we reached the bottom. I hadn't realized we had dug so deep.

"I don't see anything, soldier." It is getting dark, and my eyes aren't so good anymore.

The lieutenant takes my arm and guides me to where several lamps surround a singularity in the foundation.

The surface shines. Instead of inseparably fused elements, the cracked slab is pure white marble, broken, but not shattered. This isn't a fallen structure; it's the original roof. Had we found the top of one of the infamous monuments? Or maybe the White House itself? New life springs into my worn limbs.

"Soldier, get the drills." I still carry the case that held my equipment, and I remove the laser and begin carving away until I find the edges.

"It's not a building," I announced excitedly. "It's a monument, no, a headstone? This must be a cemetery of some kind. Three of my crew hop down to assist in cleaning off this find, their excitement contagious. It takes a while, but we finally clear enough of the surrounding junk to see the inscription. Miraculously, it is legible, and in the English language we still speak. I take out my spectacles, the same frames my grandpa had worn, and read aloud.

"Here rests in honored glory an American soldier known but to God."

A tear forms in my eye. How odd to bury someone without knowing their name. That same tear falls onto the marble, clearing away enough dust to reveal something scrawled by a knife. I identified the carving tool because part of the knife is stuck in the impression of metacarpal bones on the fossil preserved by the fused metals surrounding the tomb. A soldier, I guessed from the fragment of the helmet stuck in the concrete. The harsh scratches are more difficult to decipher. In the end, it's my Lieutenant who brushes away the dust and reads the words that echo in my brain.

We didn't sign up for this. – A loyal Patriot

The soldier had used his dying breath to write these words. Knowing the horror that was headed his way, he didn't run, he didn't desert. He took time to leave a message, the meaning of which scholars will argue about for years to come. That's when it hits me. All the people who fought the wars. The people who fought in the name of freedom for whichever country they bled for. "They didn't sign up for this."

As I repeat the words, I understand for the first time what it means to be a soldier. And I weep.

E.J. Siegler is a new writer of Science Fiction and Fantasy, sometimes all in one package. His stories blend elements of magic, technology, and human struggle, often focusing on dystopian worlds. Inspired by classic tales, modern myths, and a lifelong love of speculative fiction, he writes to share a sense of wonder and possibility. When he is not writing, E.J. spends time immersing himself in an extensive collection of Fantasy novels, gaming, and nurturing his family and their three rescue pets.

Part II: Showcase

A dazzling array of SCWG members' stand-alone short stories and book excerpts from published or upcoming works.

Book Excerpt, Nonfiction

Crawling for Connection

Julie Weissman

I scooted into the den on my tush, my shins stretching and contracting a few inches at a time to propel myself towards Mom. My wobbling head hung down. Most of my weight rested on my right hand, with my fingers only partially opened against the floor. My therapists wanted me to crawl on my hands and knees, but scooting was quicker and more efficient.

"Mommy I'm bored," I whined, sitting on the cold tiles of our hallway, my knees pointing left, and the sole of my left foot pressing into my right thigh.

"Julie, bored is not a verb. You have plenty of things to do. You can read. You can watch TV. You have a new typewriter, go write a story or something. I'm busy." Mom's tone made her irritation obvious.

"I don't want to do that. Can't we play a game?" I pleaded.

Mom swiped the newspaper against her knee. "Julie, I spent all morning with you in Hebrew school. I need to relax."

"But Mommy, I want somebody to play with me." I puckered my bottom lip, pulling tears from my eyes. "Alan and David are at their friends' houses. I want to go to Sabrina or Felicia's house. Why can't I go?"

"We need to plan for them to come for a visit. Besides, you went to Robbie's house yesterday." Mom sat on the oversized couch propping a folded newspaper on her lap and a pen in her left hand. She always played the Bridge section before doing the daily crossword puzzle.

"It's not fair. The boys can go to their friends' houses whenever they want, but I can't." I focused on another target. "Daddy, wake up. I'm bored," I said.

Dad slumped on his cotton tufted armchair. The gray tweed ottoman cushion swallowed his outstretched legs. The first time Grandma Mae tried the seat, she complained it was extremely uncomfortable. Three minutes later, she fell asleep.

"Julie, are you alright?" Dad's body shook and he blinked himself awake. A folded newspaper almost slipped from his fingers.

"I'm bored," I said. "Wake up."

"I wasn't sleeping. I was examining the inside of my eyelids." Dad waved the newspaper as he spoke.

"Alfred," Mom sighed. "You've been sawing down a forest for the last hour."

"Yeah, I heard you snoring all the way from my room. I'm bored. You promised you would take me to Carvel. Can we go now? Please." I willed my father to agree.

"A milkshake sounds good. Let me finish reading this article and then we can go." Dad picked up the *New York Times* and turned the page.

"But Daddy!" I scooted around a long wooden coffee table.

"Julie, I'll be ready in five minutes. Get in your wheelchair," Dad ordered.

"But my chair is all the way back in my room." I pointed towards the hallway.

"I guess you better start moving." Mom glanced at me and went back to scribbling on her newspaper.

I do not often have visceral reactions to my childhood memories; they project on the movie screen of my mind while I attempt to translate the imagery to written form. I'm compelled to write about boredom, or the extreme discomfort the little girl experienced on that Sunday afternoon. Remembering the isolation that my seven-year-old self-endured is physically painful. Tightness pricks the right side of my sternum where my breast begins. I ache. My chest tightens. My breath struggles to escape. My lower lip puckers. I blink back tears.

My parents didn't consider that my cries of boredom might have been cries of loneliness. The importance of social connections for students with disabilities wasn't recognized by educators until the late 1980's. Alfred and Constance Weissman were pragmatic people who encouraged me to accept life as it was, not as I wished it could be. The facts were:

- Mom and Dad were parents who needed down time on a Sunday afternoon.
- My brothers could easily spend time at their friends' homes.
- There were no friends whom I could visit.

- I rejected all mom's suggestions to relieve my boredom on my own.

The facts worked against my natural desire to be social. At age seven, I expressed my discomfort as boredom, which the Merriam-Webster Dictionary defines as "the state of being weary and restless through lack of interest." I realize all children experience boredom. However, my childhood was more complex than the dictionary implies. Yes, I felt weary and restless but, the cause was not simply a lack of interest.

In 1973, children with disabilities were educated in segregated schools. In Nassau County, students with cerebral palsy, regardless of their socioeconomic status, were bused to Roosevelt, a working-class neighborhood on the South Shore of Long Island. During the school day, my best friends and I became teachers, physical therapists, or family when we played. Sabrina had big brown oval eyes and olive skin. Her dad was American, and her mom was from Korea. Physically, we were complete opposites; her limbs were rigid while mine flew freely. Sabrina and I always got the highest scores on the state- mandated tests. Felicia made the third in our trio. I remember her dark skin, black eyes, and the multi-colored balls tightly braided in her kinky hair. Felicia used crutches to walk, and when she sat down her disability seemed to disappear.

At that tender age, I didn't grasp the differences of my classmates' lives outside of the Cerebral Palsy Center. Once an adult, I realized my good fortune in coming from a family of wealth and social status. Sabrina's dad was a mechanic, and her mom spoke limited English. Felicia didn't have a dad, and her mom earned minimum wage as a waitress. Mothers like

Sabrina's didn't always have access to prenatal care and therefore were twice as likely to have a child with cerebral palsy.

Sabrina and Felicia lived in towns far from Roslyn. Although we went to school together for eight years, I don't remember ever visiting their homes. Our physical disabilities made an ordinary playdate challenging to coordinate. If only one parent was home, feeding both Sabrina and me might be burdensome. Felicia's ability to walk meant her home was not equipped for a wheelchair, making it impossible for me to visit.

Outside school-related events, my parents didn't socialize with families from my school. Mom and Dad's closest friends belonged to our synagogue or lived in our neighborhood. Roslyn schools were not racially or economically diverse. Discriminatory housing practices and high property prices meant homeowners in East Hills were mostly white. Their children went to the same school as Alan and David whose friends lived in our neighborhood. Arranging their playdates simply required one parent to call another for details of drop off and pick up. When Mom and Dad entertained families from my brothers' schools, playtime happened spontaneously.

Since black infants were more likely to have cerebral palsy than white infants, my school was racially diverse.

I now understand that circumstance ensured that I'd never have the same easy childhood friendships my brothers had.

Segregation forced me and my family to live in two different realities. My school community was physically and socially distant from my home. No one recognized the toll this took on a seven-year-old girl.

Julie Weissman Steinbaugh—writer, advocate and mom, lives in Las Vegas. Born with cerebral palsy, she spent her life navigating a world not designed for her, all while challenging stereotypes and fighting for equality.
She serves on Nevada's Statewide Independent Living Council, working to ensure equal opportunities for people with disabilities. When not writing or advocating she enjoys her vibrant Las Vegas community.

After a short career at the IRS, the youngest inspector general in the history of the NYC Department of Investigation is in trouble immediately. He doesn't have the training or the backing for his job, the mobster he's known since childhood is his main opposition, and the office is bugged. Yet he insists on doing his job without fear or favor no matter where that leads.

They Call Me Creds

Excerpt from Chapter One

Ben Parris

1

"Responsibility is a heavy responsibility!"
– Cheech Marin, *Cheech and Chong's Next Movie*

September 25, 1989

Hoping to be first into the downtown Manhattan office, I counted the empty elevator as a good sign that no one wanted to work so early. Then I could dance on my desk, spin in my chair, and howl in victory. At age twenty-eight, I'd swapped my Revenue Agent job at the U.S. Treasury to become one of the Inspectors General for New York City's Department of Investigations. The youngest.

Don't be too impressed. There were fifty people with that title. Every department had one. But if you asked my wife, Linda, the higher pay would be a great boost for our newly minted marriage. As a bonus, I could shed the annoying nickname "Creds" in a place where I'd start fresh. Yes, I'd still have a wallet with credentials, but no one would know the embarrassing story.

Around the next turn, an empty corridor awaited, its walls covered in notices no one read. Batting a thousand as I trotted to the end. Not that the IG job would be pleasant. If there were kids who dreamed of rooting out entrenched corruption in Parks and Recreation, I never met them. Yet here I was, pretending to be the white knight of fall foliage.

Unfortunately, Senior Investigator Garold "Gary" Pinchon, who I had met during interview number two, had taken an earlier train. He swiveled in his seat to glare at me, his tie askew. "Shapiro the Hero. What are you dressed up for?"

Trying to hypnotize him to sleep, I said, "For work, Gary. I get dressed for work." Actually, I had a few new suits made at Dunlop and Speigel, where plain clothes cops went to get jackets tailored to fit over a shoulder holster. I wore the best of them, a tan pinstripe, because I had my tenth high school reunion right after work. Not that my plans were Gary's business.

"We don't dress like pansies at DOI," he said, pitching his pen at my pants, making me jump back before it made a mark. "Try the gay bar down the street."

Considering this asshole worked for me, we were off on the wrong foot. Even though his bone structure was a double extra-large, with his gun in easy reach, I leaned in with false bravado and spoke quietly. "Is there anything else you want to say to me? Garold? Because this would be the time for you to get it all out before I cross the room and take my seat behind the desk in my office. Before I remember who I am and who you are."

His eyes dropped for a moment, and I hoped mine would be the last word. To my surprise, he said, "Yeah, I have something to say. You have no business being here. I know how to run this place, and I'm not taking orders from you or giving you my case summaries. I don't want you fucking them up." In advance, I had asked the admin to have the full set of case summaries from the staff stacked on my desk. This request pleased the commissioner, making him think I knew what I was doing.

I stared at Gary for a beat, trying to think of something that would make him less certain that he could intimidate me. I opted for, "That's a big boy decision, Garold. I don't think you're up to it." I walked away, gaze steady on the aisle so I wouldn't trip. Glancing through my open door, I noticed that none of the files I'd requested sat on my desk.

At my back, he called out, "Listen, Shapiro, you're only here because you're expendable. As soon as you step in shit, Sitwell puts me in."

I rounded on him, face hot, teeth bared. "There's a good reason they didn't put you in."

Let him chew on that. If he wanted to fight, I'd clock him before he got all the way to his feet.

His eyes widened. Now we both seemed to have privileged information, the only difference being, mine was supposition.

Gary licked his lips and turned the page on his appointment book like he didn't want to take our dispute to the mat. As I hung in place to emphasize my dominance, another investigator, Pete Merrium, swung through the glass door and raised his chin in calculation. "Oh wow, I missed something good, didn't I?"

Without looking at either of us, Gary shrugged on his jacket and left.

A second later, I heard a voice echo in the hall. "You're not going anywhere." Gary re-entered, walking backwards.

Leander Sitwell stiff-armed him a good five paces. Then the boss faced into the room, eyes twinkling. "Playtime's over, children. We caught a homicide."

My hair stood on end. Homicide had never come up in the job interview. I'd heard something about DOI murder investigations on the news many years earlier. This was the only way I knew the office sometimes handled these. To say that I was in over my head was an understatement.

Sitwell turned to me, intensely curious. "Who are you assigning to this, Danny?"

Not knowing anyone's experience in the office, I bit my lip. "Can I know something about the situation first?"

"If you do your job, you're going to tell *me* what it's about."

Gary laughed loudly.

Sitwell threw a sharp glance at him. "That little chuckle just cost you the case. Now you're dismissed. And since Merrium is the only other agent here, the up goes to him." He winked at me. "See how easy this is?"

Thoroughly vexed, Gary said, "I want to stay and listen in."

Sitwell turned as if surprised to see him. "Are you still here?"

We waited while Gary left without another word, fighting with the heavy door.

I said, "Two questions. Who died, and what makes this a DOI case?"

Sitwell smiled. "Because I'm efficient, I'll give you one answer that covers both. The decedent is a Parks Department employee who filed a corruption complaint with us."

Connecting the dots, I said, "The guy must have gotten killed for his trouble."

Before I could ask another question, Sitwell handed me a slip with the location. "Lights and sirens, boys. It's bad manners to show up after the body is gone."

2

"I picked you for the job,
not because I think you're so darn smart,
but because I thought you were a shade less dumb than the rest of the outfit."
-Barton Keys, *Double Indemnity* (1944)

"Have you been on a lot of these?" I asked, trying to get my air from the window. I hate breathing in the new car smell, knowing it's all toxic chemicals.

Pete concentrated on his driving, relying on vehicles to

move aside when they saw the flashers, sometimes encouraging them with tailgating and the horn. Although we took his Geo Metro, he claimed not to know where the siren switch was. I think he found his way more entertaining.

"A lot of these what?" He shrugged. "The fact it's a Parks guy or a complaint guy will turn out to be a coincidence. They always are."

"I ask because I haven't had any training in homicide yet."

He glanced at me a little too long. "That's the DOI way. You were hired off-cycle, in a hurry. Doesn't matter. We let the police handle these things. *They* know what they're doing."

I cleared my throat. "But *you've* been to the training, right?"

"That's what I learned at training. Hang back."

It took me a little while to digest this revelation. For some reason Pete had taken Fourth Avenue on our way to Central Park and this took us alongside a green patch of Union Square, which was packed on a warm day. The shawarma carts were doing a brisk business, making me nervous when the customer line spilled into the gutter. We nearly ran over a man's foot.

"Here's what I want you to do, Pete: Get a copy of the complaint and develop your own suspects, regardless of who the police want to look at. They're going to make it out to be random violence or a mugging. Make sure you get a search warrant for the guy's apartment." I paused for him to acknowledge me.

Abruptly, Pete swerved around a sluggish car and got back in his lane just as a pigeon thumped off the windshield on my side. Didn't faze him. "You know you didn't have to come, right? They're gonna be annoyed there's two of us."

"Let them," I said. "I have to see how this works."

When we finally got to the park, we took the 65th Street Transverse, made a hard right at the East Drive restricted access path, and stopped with the car's nose touching the yellow tape.

A uniform pivoted towards us, waving frantically. "Go back."

We plastered our badges to the car window and someone in plain clothes yelled, "Let them in."

Quickly, we crossed the grass to the crime scene, me unsuccessfully pretending I wasn't bewildered at the activity. The plain clothes who pointed to where we were allowed to walk, introduced himself as Detective Rise. He was maybe forty, sandy hair, blue eyes. I found myself comparing the fit of his jacket to mine, but he didn't notice. "Thanks for coming. You're not welcome here."

"Aren't you the one who called us?" I asked with a tilt of my head.

Rise signed something on a clipboard quickly yanked back by a subordinate. "Pro forma, so you have no complaint later. Far as I'm concerned, you're a leper."

I glanced at Peter for an explanation. He leaned in and whispered, "There's an allegation, the police rookies are cheating on their exams."

"Why is that my problem?"

"They don't like we've been invited to look into it.

Especially on top of Internal Affairs. Everyone's on their backs."

"Ah. Got it." I said to Rise, "I want to see the body."

His eyes bulged. "Are you for real? Did you not hear what I just told you?"

"Pro forma," I echoed. "Your cooperation goes on the paperwork."

I PINCHED THE top of my nose and followed the detective to the tarpaulin with Pete silent for once, hanging close by my side. No way in hell I wanted to see the dead body that I just demanded to see. My last job, as an IRS agent, did not include me examining murdered civil servants staining the grass in Central Park. All I meant to accomplish on this outing was to make sure the police report wouldn't end up falsified.

Detective Rise had a word with the medical examiner out of my earshot. Then he said to me, "I'm passing you off. No need to see me after."

Our new host squatted by the body and peeled the cover back. "I know that New York City attracts a lot of tourists."

"The victim wasn't a tourist," I said.

"I mean you. The least you could have done was show up when I was explaining this the first time."

I showed my badge and said, "Let's start over. Shapiro and Merrium, DOI."

He cast a tense eye over me. "Warren Hernandez. With all due respect, I've never seen anyone from your office indulge in visiting a crime scene."

"Then we're doing something right for a change. Name of the decedent?"

"You don't even know his name?"

I nudged Pete. "Take notes, that's Warren Hernandez helping us out."

With a little smile, Hernandez said, "Don't get huffy with me. I'm all you've got. Our victim is Enji Okino, Parks Department." He paused. "Oh, now I get it. You're the new guy at DOI Parks."

"What makes you say that?"

"You've got a nasty admin in your section. Talks about you to my wife. She's in the building. Anyway, cause of death is blunt force trauma. That's how I know you're not going to stay on this case."

Pete and I exchanged a glance.

"Take a look," said Hernandez. He tilted Okino's head and the whole back of his skull came away.

I squeezed my eyes shut and held my vomit down. "How does that—mmpf. Sorry."

"And here." He showed us a bloody chunk of concrete. "We don't have an evidence bag that can hold it. I have my assistant out looking."

"And your point is?"

"Well, that chunk was once part of the curb. Separated who-knows-when? The assailant would have found it and picked it up right over there. It's the stupidest murder weapon possible and the victim's pockets are empty, indicating robbery. The killing can't be premeditated and therefore it can't be related to your guy being a whistleblower. His murder and employment are just a coincidence."

"Ha," said Pete, nudging me back. "What'd I tell you?"

3

"Ohhh, we're telling the truth."
-*The Big Chill* (1983)

The rest of my workday sucked as thoroughly as the first part. When I got back to the office, Collette Riggs, our admin, pointed out that there was, in fact, one thin file on my desk. Someone had lost it, and "as yet" she couldn't figure out who it belonged to. "As for the rest of the case summaries," she said, "you'll have to ask each individual. They're prickly about it."

Yes, I could see that from the business with Gary. "How many people work for me, Collette?"

"Can't say."

"Why not?"

"Six official. Two more on loan. One pending transfer in. Three pending transfer out."

"That comes back to six."

"If you say so. And there's some kind of deadline mentioned in that lost case, so you need to figure it out fast." A tired looking lady of about thirty, Collete had a deadpan delivery that said she had given up early.

Hoping to be friendly and motivate her, I said, "Thanks. Most people would not have checked for that issue or given me a heads up."

She narrowed her eyes. "Go fuck yourself. I was going to

do the homicide paperwork for you. Now I'm not."

I took this to mean she wasn't in the mood to be motivated.

Noting Gary's continued absence, and seeing an otherwise full house of five agents, I hopped on an empty desk, sat in the middle, and launched into an impromptu speech about what a great family we were going to be. Their reactions ranged from boredom to discomfort. A man twice my age sipped a juice box with dead eyes. Reading the room, and wondering if they treated everyone this way, I asked, "What happened to my predecessor?"

A dark blonde lady with Gothic eye shadow raised her hand.

"Yes?" I prompted her. "Ms.—?"

"Yeah, Filly Baxter." She held up one finger while she took the gum out of her mouth. "Our last IG, Cordell James, was pushed off a subway platform."

I sucked in air as my stomach dropped. "Was he…?"

"Killed? No. He made it to a platform alcove. Or almost. The train struck him in the butt, and he bashed his head into the wall. Early retirement."

"What did he say happened?"

"Doesn't want to talk about it. The last thing he said was that we were going to be a great family here, or some bullshit like that."

I opened my mouth, but nothing came out.

"Kidding," she said. "About the last part. He said we were going to be fucking warriors, and no one would stand in our way. But your dopey little speech was cute."

Ben Parris' writing took two sometimes-ironic paths, following his passions as a futurist and government reformer: speculative fiction and historical fiction in the ages of Reagan and Rome. In the first volume, *Creds: The I.R.S. Adventure*, a state senator plots to kill an IRS agent who chose to accept an assignment to audit the rich and powerful.

This is a snippet from Wayne Turmel's seventh novel, and fourth historical work, The Deserter- a Tale of the Foreign Legion. It was published January 15, 2026.

The Deserter

Wayne Turmel

Marseille, January 1908

January in Marseille was warmer than back in England but still too bloody cold to be standing in shirtsleeves waiting for sunrise. The hulking form of Fort St. Jean blocked out the moonlight, and the thick darkness swallowed even the shadows.

The big man stomped his feet, slapped and rubbed his arms to get warm. Then he ran his tongue over his top lip. For the first time in years, all he felt was smooth skin. The moustache that was such a part of him was gone, as was most of the thick blond hair that earned him the nickname Gilbert le Lion.

This lion was being hunted and needed to stay alert for a few more hours if it wanted its freedom. A clean shirt, some underwear, and his good shaving razor were all he carried in a canvas rucksack slung over his shoulder. A second razor, the sharper one, hid tucked into his boot. For the hundredth time, Gil checked that the money was still in his pocket. It was.

For now.

The sound of footsteps scuffling from the narrow alley drove him against the wall. A figure emerged and looked around. The well-dressed man was smaller than Gil, but most Frenchmen were. He wore a wool beret, a thick coat with a sweater underneath, and carried a walking stick. Anyone would think he was a merchant or a lawyer, out too late and easy pickings for street thugs.

Gil knew better.

Alert to his surroundings, the man knew someone was there, he just couldn't be sure who it was. He gave a simple, cautious nod and continued scanning the street.

Gil smiled. Vincente had come but didn't recognize him. With luck, nobody else would either.

"A guy could freeze his arse off waiting for you," Gil whispered in French. After all this time, he spoke the language well, but there was no hiding the north of England in his accent.

"*Mon Dieu*, - thought you were someone else." The older man froze, then took two tentative steps forward. "What in Christ's name did you do to yourself?" Vincente waved a finger at Gil's hairless face.

The Englishman took his friend's elbow and pulled him into a doorway. "I don't have much time, but - needed to see you."

"Has Colette seen this? She's not going to like it."

"She doesn't know. And she won't, because I'm leaving. This morning. That's why I needed to see you."

Gil shuddered and expelled a breath, visible in the chilly night air. The older man instinctively offered his coat. The Englishman shook him off.

"I'm fine. The sun will be up soon."

"What do you mean, you're leaving?"

Gil ignored the question. "How much do you owe The Belgian?"

Vincente sighed. "Too much. What is it now, a hundred thousand? Not enough to kill me for, too much to let it slide. He threatens and I ask for more time. It's a game."

Gil reached into his pocket and grabbed a wad of crumpled bills the size of his fist, wrapped in a rubber band. "A game you can't win. Get him off your back. My gift to you. For… well, for everything." He shoved it towards his friend.

"Vincente recoiled. "What's that? Jesus, boy, where did that come from?"

Gil shrugged. "Does it matter?"

"Of course it matters."

Ignoring the protest, Gil grabbed his friend's wrist and placed the money in his palm, closing the fingers over it. "I'm done. For good. Just paying my debts."

The sky was becoming lighter over the Mediterranean. Four-thirty maybe. He needed to stay invisible until eight thirty at most. Four long hours.

"You don't owe me anything," Vincente said weakly.

"I owe you pretty much everything. Now we're square, and you can tell The Belgian to *embrasse ton cul*. With my compliments."

Somewhere on the next street, a door slammed, and a cat yowled as Marseille awoke. The city dawned grumpy and mean. "Where are you going?" Vincente asked.

"Away. From Marseille, from all this. I can't live this way anymore."

Vincente studied the younger man's face for far too long. Finally, he looked down and saw the bloodstains on the tail of Gil's shirt. "You're hurt."

Gil tucked the shirt in, hiding most of the blood. "It's not mine."

"Then whose…" Vincente stopped. His face and voice turned to stone. "The card game in La Barasse. That was you?" He turned away and checked for eavesdroppers down the alley. "Do they know?"

Gil held his palms up, pleading for him to be quiet. "By now? Probably. Likely. After today it won't matter."

Vincente's eyes were watery. "What's that mean after today? You're not going to, you know. You promised never to do that again."

Gil remembered that last half-hearted attempt, and his thumb traced the scar on his left wrist unconsciously. Like everything he'd done since arriving in Marseille, the act was more messy than effective and laid a heavy burden on the few people who cared. Colette nursed him. Vincente gave him a place to recover and a job. No, he wouldn't do that to them again.

But he desperately needed to leave. Marseille. The petty hustles. The ever-present threat of childish, pointless violence. He needed order back in his life. Couldn't survive without it another day. There was still one place, and only one, he could get it. If he could make it to sunrise. The morning could not come fast enough.

While Gil was lost in thought, Vincente unwrapped the money and expertly thumbed through it. "Paying him back with his own money. You've got balls, I'll say that." He took two bills between his fingers and held them out. "There's too much. At least keep some for yourself. "

"Give it to Colette." The name stuck in his throat.

The older man tried shoving the hundred-franc notes into Gil's hand, but it was balled into an impenetrable fist. "You'll need it."

"Not where I'm going."

Vincente tried to look into his eyes. "And where's that, pray tell?"

Gil motioned with his head to the fort behind them. In the coming dawn, guards were visible, pacing on the parapet and in front of the giant wooden gate.

His friend squinted, confused. Then his eyes grew wide. "Bullshit." Gil shrugged.

"It would be faster to just kill yourself."

"I need to do this."

"I don't get it," Vincente said, his voice full of fatherly concern.

"I know, mate."

The early morning sounds and sights of the city filled the air. Water lapped against the boats at their moorings. Horses clip-clopped on stones, dragging squeaky carts. Gas lamps appeared in upper windows.

"At least let me buy you breakfast?"

Gil smiled. "Probably the last decent meal I'm going to have for a long time. Sure. But somewhere dark."

Vincente slapped his fingers against the bloodstains on the

big man's shirt. "You'll need a fresh shirt. Can't show up like hell. Even they won't ignore something like that."

"Feed me first, then you can nag me."

Breakfast was delicious, the jam sweet, the croissants flaky and the air full of smoky bacon and companionable silence. They sat in the corner near the kitchen, smoking and drinking coffee. As old friends do, they avoided any talk of parting or where Gil was headed. It was the nicest morning Gil had experienced in far too long. And it would be the last of its kind.

Eventually, they stood on the sidewalk in front of the cafe. Gil looked everywhere but the port, while Vincente avoided meeting his eyes. Finally, the Englishman stuck his hand out. "Adieu, my friend. Thank you."

"Crazy bastard." Vincente stuck two notes into the offered hand, then shook it and pulled him in for a bear hug. "Au revoir, Gilles."

Without dragging it out another second, Gil stuffed the money into his pocket, turned and walked with determination towards the port and Fort St. Jean. He felt Vincente watching, so he turned the corner a block too early just to be out of sight.

That nearly proved fatal. Two large goons stood at the top of the concrete stairs leading down to the docks. They smoked and watched the street, waiting for anyone trying to escape by boat. it was too much to hope The Belgian hadn't recognized him. Now he had to avoid these two gorillas.

It was just for a bit more. He could do it. He had to. The clean shirt in his bag was identical to the one he had on, minus the obvious evidence of his crime. It wouldn't provide any sort of disguise. Everyone knew the Lion was a creature of habit, always wearing the same thing every day. Even half-shorn, they'd recognize him in an instant.

Gil considered the matter of his blood stained shirt. He needed to change his appearance. Fast. Turning back a few blocks, he leaned against a cold stone wall to think.

The sound of retching drew his attention. A man just a little smaller than himself was puking into the gutter. A drunken sailor was stumbling back to his ship from a night in one of Marseille's most decrepit brothels. The Italian snatched Gil's last twenty francs and swapped them for his watch cap and striped sweater. They were a size too small for Gil's sturdy frame but would suffice.

As the man everyone knew as Gilbert le Lion pulled the fetid shirt on, he glimpsed his reflection in a bakery window. The sailor's shabby blouse bulged at the gut and stretched around Gil's thick neck and wrists. He'd never be caught wearing such rags, and his pursuers knew it. Perfect.

The morning dawned gray and chilly. Gilbert stood on the opposite side of the cobblestone street staring at the fort, then turned west away from the rising sun. For the last time, he took in the city that had been home but nearly destroyed him.

Out of a long-lost habit, he stiffened his back and marched with arms swinging to the small office building next to the fort. He lifted his leg and stomped to a halt. Gilbert studied the faded sign on the wall.

"La Légion Etrangère." The Foreign Legion.

Underneath it in smaller print, it simply said, *"Enrôlement."* Enlistment.

He reeked of failure, sweat, and another man's whore, but

it couldn't be helped. Chin up and eyes clear, Gilber tossed the cap in the gutter and stepped inside.

BRITISH, FRENCH, it didn't matter. All military offices smelled the same.

Because the windows were closed against the chilly wind off the harbor, the air was stale and dead. Tobacco smoke penetrated the walls like creosote and streaked the windows. The furniture smelt of sweat and flatulence, not to mention the desperation of those sitting on it.

He took a deep breath. His heart missed a beat.

Two people looked up to see him enter. One was a nervous-looking kid, maybe twenty years old. He wore a working man's clothes. At his feet was a brand-new travel bag. A gift from a worried parent? Gil had owned one just like it before he set off for the depot at seventeen. He couldn't help but feel a tinge of sympathy for the youngster. Had he ever been so young and innocent?

He barely remembered sitting in that chair in Newcastle. Certainly, his old man hadn't given him anything but a black eye.

Across a trestle table, the second man tapped his pencil to get the young man's attention. The sergeant's pinched Gallic face scrunched as if a whiff of sulfur had blown in. His perfect uniform was out place in such a shabby room but gave him an unmistakable air of superiority. As intended. The way his left hand hung limply at his side explained his presence in France.

He saw Gil and gestured with a pointed nose to a wooden

chair against the far wall.

With a curt, "je *m'excuse, sergent,*" Gil took a chair. He sat ramrod straight, hands on his knees like a good soldier. Three years of indolence and spitting at authority surrendered to muscle memory in a second. He allowed himself a brief smile.

"Very well. All we need is for you to sign your name here, if you know how, and you are a part of the Foreign Legion. It's all here- a term of five years. Five centimes a day, payable monthly minus the cost of your uniform."

Gil Flinched. Her Majesty's army paid new recruits a shilling a day; five times what was being offered. He knew the Legion's pay was low, and in the depths of the desert, hard currency was practically useless. But after so much easy access to cash, he felt his guts tighten. Maybe that was because the kid was obviously green and coming in at the lowest rank. Gil could get a better deal. The money was secondary, but a man had to eat.

"Sign here with your *nom de guerre*. You will only be known by this name, and you'll renounce your French citizenship for the first year."

"What's wrong with my real name?"

Gil knew the question identified the young man as cannon fodder. He imagined that baby face covered in snot and tears the first time a sergeant bawled him out. Like his had been and he survived. Maybe the kid would be alright.

Maybe not.

"You want to be the same good little French boy you were when you walked in? Join the army. In the Legion, you aren't not French or anything other than a soldier. Odds are you won't live long enough to regret it. If you do, you'll earn your citizenship back. Sign it. Or don't."

Gil winced at the callous tone but watched intently. With shaking hands, the kid took a pen from the officer. He scrawled a new name across the paper then dropped the pen. The officer pulled the paper across the desk, read it, rose to his feet and extended his hand.

"Jean LaForce. Welcome to the Legion"

The newly minted LaForce stared at the empty hand for a second, then grabbed it with unnecessary force. He squeezed hard, as they taught in school and pumped it twice. As an afterthought, he gave a semblance of a salute.

"Do you have somewhere to stay tonight?"

"*Oui, Sergent*. My uncle lives in town."

"We muster at dawn. Report with your papers and one bag of belongings."

LaForce stood dumbly until the recruiter pointed to the door. He nodded and picked up his bag. "Of course, see you tomorrow, sir."

The older man sneered. "Like hell you will. You think I'm going to that shithole with you? I will stay in France with the wine and the white women. Adieu."

The kid turned and smiled at Gil. He extended his hand. "Jacques Manot."

"You mean LaForce." Gil enjoyed the confused look on the youngster's face." It's a good name, LaForce. Means strong. Ballsy. I like it, but you'd better get used to it. Try again."

A blush warmed the boy's barely shaven cheeks. Christ, there's no way he'd ever been so young and innocent.

"Of course. Jean LaForce. You are?"

"I don't know yet. In a few minutes it won't matter. It

sounded cold, but he hoped the kid would take the hint and leave.

Out of the corner of his eye, he saw the recruiter point to the chair. “If you’re done flirting, you’re next.”

Wayne Turmel has been a member of SCWG since October of 2018. To learn more, visit www.WayneTurmel.com

The Costume of Death

Erik Engman

Guthrum the Executioner stood back admiring his handiwork. Hanging in front of him was a sign dripping with fresh paint that read "The Tower of London First Annual Costume Contest 1598."

He adjusted his outfit for the umpteenth time. Fancy dress never suited him, especially the itchy neck ruff. He much preferred the loose clothing and hood of his executioner uniform. But comfort be damned, he was certain that with this garb he would win the contest.

"Is crooked," came a meek voice from behind.

Guthrum winced at the whinging in his ears and turned to find the guard, Basil, staring at the sign, head tilted to one side. He swung his hand at the sentry, barely missing him. "You'll be crooked when I'm finished with ya. Now get yer' self back in line with the others."

Focusing his attention to the rest of his motley mix of employees, Guthrum couldn't help but feel depressed. There was, of course, Basil, scurrying back into line like a rat who's about to be a cat's dinner. Then the large oaf of a man, Digby, who was occupied by picking lint from the belly button on his enormous gut. Then there was the erratic, wiry Nigel, who constantly fidgeted as if he had a turnip in his trousers. And last, but not least, was Tuppence, the dim-witted tea lady.

Guthrum cleared his throat. "Hear ye! Hear ye! Let the First Annual Halloween Costume Contest commence!"

"What does holler'ween mean?" asked Digby, nonplussed as usual.

Tuppence replied, "Dearie, it's a holiday that we get to holler at people."

"Master Guthrum celebrates that every day!" laughed Nigel.

Guthrum rolled his eyes. "Halloween, for yer information, is a day to ward off evil spirits."

"I need that," said Basil, holding his tummy. "I drank too much evil spirits last night at the Queen's Fiddle pub."

"Not *those* kind of spirits, ya dolt," said Guthrum. "Spirits of the spectral kind. Now let's present our costumes. The winner gets a box of sweets."

Nigel jumped up and down. "I love sweets!"

"Donit think you need more sugar, Nigel," observed Guthrum. "Now then, who's first?"

Digby lumbered forward. His raised hand was covered by a muddy sock.

"And what are you supposed to be?" Guthrum asked.

"I'm a snake, aren't I?" said Digby. "Hold on. Fergot something." He rummaged in his pocket with his free hand and pulled out two, squishy, bloody eyeballs, balancing them on top of the sock. "Hissss...," he said, moving the snake in a figure eight.

"*Very* impressive," said Basil.

"Where'd ya get them eyeballs from?" asked Guthrum.

"Peter the Pig Stealer."

Tuppence sighed and dreamily looked at the sock. "Oh, I loved that man's eyes. They were so glamorous, popping out of his head when we hung him up from the rafters."

Nice attempt, Digby," said Guthrum. "Next up?"

Basil opened a small satchel. "Hold on! Let me get ready!" He pulled out a soiled sheet and threw it over his head. "Go on. Who'd ya think I am?"

"A bedbug?" asked Guthrum.

"No, silly! I'm a ghost! I cut out eye holes and everything." Basil let out a loud moan.

"I didn't realize ghosts stank so much," said Gunthum, holding his nose.

"Maybe it's one of them Polter-ghosts?" offered Nigel.

"I don't quite see it," pondered Guthrum. "I just hope the missus don't clobber ya for cutting up the linen."

"I'm next! I'm next!" exclaimed Nigel, his arm high up in the air.

"Go on, then," said Guthrum.

Nigel just stood there, his arms outstretched. "Well? What d'ya think?"

Guthrum rubbed his stubbly jaw. "You're not wearin' a costume. That's just yer guard uniform."

"Don't you see? I'm not me. I'm Basil!" Nigel smiled wide.

Tuppence crossed her arms and nodded. "Well I'll be!"

"Uncanny," gasped Digby.

Basil stood transfixed. "It's like looking in a mirror...."

"Hmmmm," muttered Guthrum. "Tuppence, it's yer turn."

Tuppence wore a burlap sack. Dead cats were tied all around her waist. "I'm catnip, sir."

Guthrum nodded. "S'ppose you are, m'lady. S'ppose you are."

"And, please, sir, might we hurry it up a bit? I gotta get these felines over to Mrs. Pumman's Pie Shop. They're starting to go off." She scrunched her nose as the rest of the group recoiled from the smell.

"We're almost done," assured Guthrum. "One contestant left. Me!" He brushed the dust off his clothes, picked up a book, and posed with his head tilted up in a proud and lofty manner. "Well? Impressed?"

A wall of blank faces answered him.

Guthrum's shoulders dropped. "I'm the bard!"

The blank faces remained blank.

"The celebrated writer of our city of London!" he added.

The faces couldn't get any blanker.

"SHAKESPEARE! II" he yelled, slamming the book to the ground.

Basil shrugged. "We don't go to the theater, m'lord. We're more into sports."

"Pigball," said Digby, smiling.

"Pigball? Never heard of it," replied Guthrum.

Nigel danced around. "We get a wee pig and kick it back and forth until it stops running!"

"Or he bites too many people." Tuppence smiled mischievously. "I like the biting…"

"All right, all right. Have it yer way. You are all uncouth bumpkins."

"Thank you, my lord!" beamed Basil.

"It's time now to pick the winner. Who's going to get the jackpot of sweets? Who's got the best costume? I think it's obvious." Guthrum indicated his fancy clothes.

Everyone else said in unison, "Bernard!"

"Bernard? Who the heck is Bernard?"

His crew pointed up to the far wall. Hanging up by his wrists was a man's body dressed in a long gown. His head was cut off.

Basil smiled. "Bernard the Blasphemer. He wanted to participate in this contest *so* much. We promised we'd cut off his head instead of boiling him in oil."

"He was very happy with that decision," added Digby. "At least, at first."

"Who's he supposed to be, then?" asked Guthrum.

"Mary Queen of Scots," said Nigel.

Guthrum sighed, defeated. "Ya know, I agree. I tell ya what, we divvy up the sweets amongst ourselves."

"And maybe Bernard gets the best prize of them all," said Tuppence with all due reverence. "Meeting the Lord God Almighty."

Guthrum shrugged his shoulders. "Sadly, ol' Bernard prob'bly won't be up there sporting wings and playing a harp. He'll most likely be down there in everlasting torment, demons devouring his soul. And if that isn't the spirit of Halloween, then I don't know what is!"

Erik Engman lives in Las Vegas where he teaches clown and improvisation. He regularly performs with the groups 1230 Clowns and the Las Vegas Improvisation Players. He is a comedy Science Fiction and Fantasy writer. He has had four of his stories published in the anthologies *Engineering Chaos* and *Alien Gaze* for NaNoWriMo, and *Trouble in Paradise* for Dreambridge Publishing. His fourth story is coming out in January in the anthology *In My Element*, also by Dreambridge Publishing. He has also written multiple plays, scripts and grocery lists. And on top of all that he is a theater critic with EatMoreArtVegas.com .

Cold Front

Nancy E. Sherer

40 °

Willie hunched his shoulders against the wind. He didn't know where he was, but he remembered leaving the camp. For most of the summer, his home was on the edge of an industrial park under the low, sweeping branches of a fir tree. His bed roll was a bundle of old blankets wrapped in plastic. In his hurry to leave, he wadded it into his shopping cart instead of rolling it neatly like he usually did. He never took off his heavy canvas Salvation Army coat. He shivered as the cold leaked in the neck and arm holes. Instead of a cap, he had a football helmet that not only kept his head warm, but also cut out much of the noise of the street.

This morning, the police came to the camp. He didn't hang around to see what they wanted. He never pan-handled, but that wouldn't stop them from hauling him to jail. He packed up his shopping cart and headed up a trail to the sidewalk. The camp was too dangerous anyway now that the boys of summer had moved south. The couple dozen who stayed with their rain slickers and cardboard "anything helps" signs left him alone, but he didn't like their odd, sly glances at his belongings.

He didn't pay attention to where he was going until the mewing from his cart caught his attention. Stuart, a sleek, black and white cat crawled out from the rags that made its bed. Willie scooped it up and tucked it inside his coat. The cat struggled until its head peeked out just above the collar. Willie had a can of tuna somewhere in the cart, but he wanted to get away from the stores and fast-food kiosks before stopping. When he got to the knot of freeway entrances, he saw Virgil standing on the median with his "not for drugs, not for booze, need traveling money" sign. Willie knew about Virgil. He was a mean snake of a man, so Willie turned the corner to avoid him.

Now he was passing strip malls and gas stations. Sometimes people reached out with money in their hands, but he turned his head and marched on. He used his trick to be invisible, looking in the distance with his chin up. He knew that if he couldn't see them, they couldn't see him.

36 °

PATROLMAN JESICK watched Willie hunched down behind the shopping cart as the cat crawled into his coat. Willie helped the bedraggled animal cuddle in, then buttoned the parka. The shopping cart was aimed north toward River Road.

Jesick was six foot two, but Willie was bigger. He was as big as a bear and smelled worse. The last time Wille had been taken in, the patrol car stunk for a week. Still, the order of the day was to warn indigents about the cold front that was moving in. Shelters were open all over town. Unfortunately for Jesick, Willie was 10-96, mentally ill. That meant that the only way to keep the crazy bugger from freezing to death was a three-day hold in a jail cell. From there, social services could figure out what to do with him for the rest of the winter. Willie was usually meek and harmless, but that was no guarantee. Jesick decided to call for back-up.

Before he could make the call, dispatch put out an alert that an accident on the bypass would require all available officers. A fuel tanker had tipped over and was spilling gasoline. Feeling relief that he was needed elsewhere, Jesick turned the squad car around, making a mental note to take care of Willie later.

30°

STUART MEWED. Willie smelled hamburgers in his cart but didn't remember where the warm bag of food came from. He walked faster toward a road that headed to the river. Pushing the cart to where the sidewalk became a gravel path, he jockeyed it into the bushes. He was too cold to make sure that it was well hidden. A few yards down the path, fir branches swept the ground. He sat down beneath them and examined the contents of the fast-food bag. There were several hamburgers, fries, a cup of coffee and a bottle of milk. He hand-fed Stuart between gulping bites for himself.

He could make camp under the firs on the hillside, but the cart would have to stay in the weeds by the road. Stuart nestled back into his coat, the cat lining his neck like a scarf as they started down the trail with the blankets for bedding. He saw two boys at the river's edge and stared past them to make himself invisible. No telling what boys might do, and these two were crazy enough to be by the river in this cold weather, so it was better that they not see him at all.

He crawled under the grand fir's low boughs. After rolling out his bed, he nestled the cat into the folds of plastic, paper and blankets. Light was fading in the winter sky, but with those boys still around, he needed to keep watch. He circled around the trees to see what they were doing.

26°

JESICK DIDN'T GET within half a mile of the accident scene, but the sugary smell of spilled gasoline wafted by him. He was assigned to divert traffic. His winter gear kept him warm, but after two hours standing in one place breathing in the cold air, he was tired and chilled. As he waved drivers to the side road, the vision of his gas fireplace and coffee laced with bourbon drifted through his mind. His shift would be over at four, and since the incident scene was starting to clear, he might make it home before dark.

A patrol car pulled up next to him and Jack Almaso got out.

"Looks like you can head out," Jack said. "Emergency vehicles cleared most of the wreckage. The hazmat team is dealing with the fuel spill. Go get warmed up."

"Thanks. My legs are so stiff, I'll have to drive back standing up."

22°

THEY WERE SMALL, maybe not even ten years old. One of them was up farther on the bank, holding a long, skinny stick out towards the other one. The other was down the bank, almost in the water. It took a few seconds before Willie realized what was going on. The boy was on a nest of branches snagged on a fallen tree. However he had gotten there, there wasn't any way for him to get back unless he grew wings to fly. Willie considered this for a few seconds, then realized that was a crazy idea. The raft of branches bobbed up and down on the current, threatening to drift away. Willie forgot to be invisible as he slid down the bank towards the boys.

The boy on the bank was yelling something about help, but Willie ignored him. Reaching a hand out wouldn't do any good because the kid was too small to wade through the current. Stomping past the boy on the bank, Willie waded into the river. Icy water filled his boots, biting his ankles and thighs, but Willie kept his eyes on the terrified face and took another step. Then he leaned forward and picked the boy up by the back of his coat the way a mama cat would pick up a kitten. He pivoted toward the shore and carried the boy ahead of him as he climbed to dry land. Half chasing, half carrying, Willie got him up the riverbank. The other boy crawled up behind and then they scurried off.

Willie trudged back to his camp. His pants were soaked through, and the bottom part of his coat was wet. His leg muscles were already stiff when he crawled into his bedroll.

22°

JESICK STOPPED TO talk to Judy at the desk on his way out.

"Is the hazmat team finished yet?" he asked.

"It looks like they will be done before the cold front moves in." She nodded toward the employee parking lot. "Is that truck the one you spent six months' pay on?"

"Yup. Delivered yesterday, deluxe package. Who needs money when you can have leather seats?" He pulled his coat on. "Did anybody pick up Willie? He was walking north on River Road when I saw him this morning."

"Not that I know about. Maybe somebody from one of the shelters got him."

"Let's hope so. We shut down an encampment near there last spring. I hope he didn't go back."

Jesick braced himself against the cold as he walked across the parking lot to his new Silverado. The display panel on his dash glowed blue as the truck came to life. A white snowflake icon punctuated the temperature, twenty degrees. The sun slipped below the horizon. It would be dark soon.

He turned left on Commerce, then south out of town, towards his house and a warm fire. As the air in the cab warmed, he could smell the leather seats. Worth the extra money, he thought. After a long, hot shower, maybe he would invite Grace over for drinks and dinner.

He glanced at the dash. The temperature had dropped to fifteen. Five degrees in five minutes. The arctic air was moving in fast. He knew that nobody, even one with the luck of a madman, could survive outside tonight.

He caught a red light at Rosewood even though his was the only vehicle on the road. As he waited for the light to change, he took a last deep breath of the new car smell, then pulled through the intersection, making a U-turn to drive north to River Road.

An empty wire shopping cart lay next to the gravel path.

Jesick pulled over, then followed the trail of crushed weeds. A cat mewed from beneath a grand fir, and Jesick pulled out his phone for help.

Nancy E. Sherer is the author of dozens of non-fiction articles and stories, including the prize-winning short story, "Jacob's Dog." Her mid-grade action/adventure story "Snow Angels," is available on Amazon and Kindle Direct. Her latest novel, "Haunted," will be released soon. She currently lives in Las Vegas, Nevada, where she hikes the Mojave Desert trails with her dog, Sparky.

The Wolverine Boots

Kevin Keefe

Warm vapor wafted over Nate's face, carrying the stench of stale breath. He opened his eyes and saw the family dog just inches away. "Awful early today, Oz."

He reached over and squeezed his wife Jess's behind. "Wanna come?"

She groaned. "No thanks. I'm sleeping in."

Darkness still ruled, but its hold on the night grew weak. By the time he got dressed and went downstairs to the kitchen, a magenta glow had broken over the mountain.

One cup of coffee and one bowl of dog food later, they were ready to go. The Continental Divide beckoned, three and a half miles and twelve hundred vertical feet from his house on the outskirts of Helena.

A half mile from the summit, he passed through thickets of huckleberries, little green orbs plumping on the vine. Another month and they'd be ready for picking. He closed his eyes for a few seconds and imagined the sweet tang of Jess's huckleberry pie.

A fresh paw print, longer and wider than his boot, jolted him back to reality. He stopped and listened intently as he checked his surroundings. Reading the tracks, it looked like a bear had walked straight up the mountain. He couldn't tell whether it was a Grizzly or a black bear. But it had to be huge.

Since the prints led uphill, he decided to turn toward home. He called Oz who came running.

Back at the house, he stepped out of the kitchen just as his daughter Cindy dashed naked from the bathroom across the hall to her room. He averted his eyes and stifled a laugh. She'd been streaking at home ever since she could walk.

A month ago, Cindy returned from Bozeman after graduating from Montana State. Right away the house seemed warmer, cheerier.

But she'd changed, and so had he and Jess. They were earlier to bed and earlier to rise, whereas Cindy had gone nocturnal.

Some mornings she was still out from the night before when Nate came down to put the coffee on. He wondered where she went and who was this guy Drew she kept talking about?

ONE EVENING WHILE Cindy was stirring the spaghetti sauce, Nate gently squeezed her shoulder.

She jumped. "Ow!"

"Sorry. I barely touched you. Are you okay?"

"Just a bruise from playing soccer." She grimaced. "You should be more careful."

A week later, Jess was crying at the kitchen table when he came back home. "I saw Cindy fresh out of the shower. Oh, my God! She has bruises up and down her back and on her stomach. She won't say it, but I think Drew is abusing her."

Nate furrowed his brow. "Now I know why she's wearing turtlenecks and long sleeves in the middle of summer."

Jess reached out and grabbed his hand. "We need to do something."

"Let's invite Drew over for dinner," Nate said. "I'd like to take his measure."

ON THE MORNING before dinner with the boyfriend, Nate trekked up the mountain to check his berry patch. The huckleberries were starting to turn red and purple. He'd be filling buckets of them in a matter of days. Moving on, he spied something in the middle of the trail.

Bear shit!

Very fresh, still wet, and steaming in the cool mountain air. *That beast is way too close.*

Woof, woof, woof. Oz raced down the slope toward Nate and hid behind his legs. The dog continued to bark as it looked up the mountain.

Nate patted its head. "You're supposed to protect me, you big chicken. Let's get outta here before the bear comes back."

THE NEXT EVENING, Cindy brought Drew over for dinner. He wore a blue and white flannel shirt, tan Carhartt pants and brown leather boots.

Nate looked Drew over and gave a nod. "Nice shoes. Wolverines?"

"That they are. Best damn boots I ever owned."

"You should take better care of them," said Nate, eyeing the scuffed up footwear. "Anyway, please take them off and set them by the other shoes."

They sat down for drinks as they waited for dinner and opened a bottle of wine to accompany their meal.

Afterwards, Nate poured a couple bourbons and turned to Drew. "Let's relax in the living room while the women clean up."

Drew downed his drink in one gulp. "I like your style. Leave the women in the kitchen."

His words came out slurred. "My daddy always said a woman needs a firm hand."

So that's the kind of guy you are. Nate's grip on his glass tightened almost to the shattering point, but he managed to keep his composure. "I hear you loud and clear."

Drew refilled his glass and took a deep slug.

"You need to stay here tonight," said Nate. "I can't let you drive home like this."

"I think I'm okay, sir."

Nate grimaced and shook his head. "Be smart. We have an extra bed."

"Thanks. I'll stay."

"Why don't we hike up to the ridge tomorrow, I'd like to see how you handle yourself on the mountain."

"I'm a Montanan, I'm always ready."

UP IN THE BEDROOM, Jess confronted Nate. "That man is abusing our daughter and you want to cozy up to him. Have you no spine?"

Nate held up his hands. "I let him talk to see what he's all about, and found he's not worth a damn. I almost threw him out, but that wouldn't get rid of our problem."

"What are you going to do?" she asked.

"Trust me, I'll handle this. Tomorrow morning, I need you to take Cindy with you to town. Go to brunch, do some shopping or whatever. But stay away all morning."

Nate was the first one up at dawn. He pulled two pounds of bacon out of the fridge and put a large skillet on the burner. Within minutes the smoky aroma would work its way into every nostril in the house.

He poured off the grease into an old jelly jar, saving some in the pan for eggs.

Next he grabbed Drew's scruffy leather boots from the entryway and took them to the workroom for a good polishing. He rubbed grease into every nook and cranny. Soon the Wolverines were looking mighty supple. He placed them back by the other shoes and sat down at the kitchen table with a cup of coffee and his laptop.

Cindy popped in. "Smells great in here. You making eggs?" She grabbed a rasher and took a bite while looking at her dad with raised eyebrows.

"Sorry, not for you. Your mom's taking you to town. Drew and I are going to have breakfast and hike up to the ridge."

"Like I want to go traipsing through the woods with you two anyway." Cindy rolled her eyes at her dad. "You made enough bacon for a week."

Jessie came down to the kitchen and looked at her

daughter. She beckoned toward the garage. "Let's head out."

Drew came into the kitchen ten minutes later, freshly showered, but looking far from alert. He groaned and shook his head. "I drank too much last night. My whole body hurts."

'You'll feel better once you get some food in you. Why don't you get your shoes on while I scramble up some eggs. That way we can head out right away."

"Sounds good. I woke up dreaming of bacon," said Drew as he walked toward the door.

"Holy cow! My boots look great." He sat down at the table with a steaming cup of coffee and put on his shoes.

Nate, lost in thought, hardly said a word as he dug into his breakfast.

About a mile into the trek, Nate stepped awkwardly over a rock and fell to the ground. "Damn it! I twisted my ankle."

He slowly stood up and winced when his right foot touched the ground. "I need to go back, but you should keep going. The view from the summit is worth the effort. Do me a favor and take a picture at the top. If you can make it that far."

Drew puffed up his chest, arms akimbo. "Like I said last night, I'm a Montanan. You'll get your photo."

NATE CHECKED HIS phone for what felt like the hundredth time when the girls returned home in the afternoon. Still no pictures.

"Where's Drew?" asked Cindy.

He forced himself to look her in the eye. "Still on the mountain. I came back after twisting my ankle, but he was set on reaching the summit. Come to think of it, he's been up there a while."

What began as sirens in the distance, kept growing increasingly louder as emergency vehicles passed their house. They watched the flashing lights go by. "I wonder who that's for," said Jess. "There's only four more houses up this way."

"Let's report Drew missing, just to be safe," said Nate. "They should know he's up there."

He called 911 and explained that Drew had not returned from the forest where the emergency teams were now headed.

At three PM, a Fish Wildlife and Parks truck crunched up the gravel driveway. A uniformed ranger wearing a straw cowboy hat came to the door and introduced himself. "Are you the one who called and reported a missing hiker?"

"Yes," said Nate. "Drew Harvey started off from here headed toward the ridge. Been gone about six hours now."

"I'm sorry to inform you that a bear killed your friend."

Cindy screamed and ran to her room sobbing, followed by her mother.

The game warden pulled out his phone. "Let me show you a picture just to make sure we have the right guy."

Nate looked at a close up of Drew's face with his unseeing eyes wide open.

He pursed his lips and nodded. "That's him alright."

The man swiped right and a full length pic of the body came up. Drew's abdomen was torn open by claw marks and one of the boots was missing. Nate sucked in his breath and rubbed his face. The whole damn foot was gone.

THAT EVENING NATE grilled on the deck out back. He took the bacon grease soaked rag he used for polishing the boots and threw it on the burning coals. He savored the aroma as it crackled and burst into flames.

Then he looked around to make sure nobody was watching before he danced a vigorous jig on his newly recovered ankle.

Omelettes and Curses

Leah Churchville

I took a different route to avoid the torrential flooding on Boulder Highway; unfortunately, everyone else seemed to have the same idea. Idling in traffic, I thought of my recent windfall as I stared at my lucky rabbit's foot dangling from the rear-view mirror. The good luck charm was kind of gross if I thought about it, but it still brought me comfort.

An accident ahead, undoubtedly caused by some poor schmuck not used to driving in the rain. It would take a while to get around it, so I impulsively turned, taking a shortcut down some side streets to avoid the congestion and shave off time. A larger vehicle, maybe an SUV, from the same lane, followed suit.

I hadn't had a first date in a while, and being late wasn't the tone I wanted to set with her. She was out of my league, and I was surprised she said yes to a guy like me. Only brave enough to ask jokingly, I gave her an out, and I thought she'd laugh it off, but she agreed to the date with a huge smile. This was before I even knew about the windfall. I still hadn't told her about the money, so her interest in me might be legit.

She'd been patient, having to wait to go on our date until after I dealt with all the funeral and legal hoops. Sympathetic even.

The streets were darker here, and through the swipes of the wipers, people and cars were scarcer. I braked early at the third intersection since the roads were still slick, stopping with plenty of room.

Slam!

A rear-end collision. After the initial shock, I conducted a brief inventory using the heads, shoulders, knees, and toes method to be sure I was okay. My neck ached, and my shoulder burned from the seatbelt, but hopefully, that was the extent of it.

Either way, it's official; I'll live.

The impact was hard enough to slide my car right into the intersection. Thankfully, no one was coming. I drew a deep breath to calm my rattled nerves and quell the flash of anger that came. I'm not an aggressive guy and didn't plan on unleashing my anger on the driver who just uglified my beautiful midnight-blue baby.

Okay, technically, she wasn't mine yet. Ordered as a "company car," the Dodge Hellcat was on loan until probate cleared. Being late to the lawyers' meetings because I had to take the bus didn't sit well with anyone, including the interim director. So, two days ago, a week after they told me to choose something "modest", they gave me a new car.

I'd never owned a brand-new car, let alone such a perfect beauty. I had to pinch myself looking at her satin-finished exterior, sans graphics or badges; I'm no street racer and didn't want to be challenged every time I stopped at a light. A modest purchase compared to what I could soon afford, the glorified four-door sedan didn't cost any more than the Lincolns the law firm usually ordered. At least that's how the guy from the company's finance department justified approving the muscle car purchase.

I rubbed my aching neck gingerly as I breathed, remembering to be thankful.

The light was obviously red; they'd better be frigging insured.

Stop it, Scrooge McDuck. You'll be fine.

Okay… but it's a matter of principle.

Learn to give some grace; you can afford it.

After arguing with myself like I had the haloed and horned ones literally on my shoulders, I said one last "whoosah" and cracked open my door, leaving the engine running. The scent hit me, and I breathed in the rain, loving the smell of ozone in the air.

Drops pelted my face, and I pulled the forgotten hood of my jacket up loosely over my head, wiping water from my eyes as I headed back to check on the driver. They hadn't even opened a door, but I was still blinded by their lights and the rain. It was impossible to see anyone through the windows of the SUV.

Ignoring the shiver from the cold rainwater that rolled down my neck, I squinted; it seemed they were reaching out a hand from the window to wave that they were alright.

Relieved, I smiled and raised my hand halfway when I was startled by a lightning strike, a quick, blinding flash of light followed by immediate thunder.

I flinched. "Shit! That was close!" I exclaimed under my breath as the memory of how the timing for thunder works popped into my head.

Oddly, the flash of light seemed localized, right in front of me, and I registered a buzz whistling past my ear.

I don't know *how* I knew, but a part of my brain screamed, 'Gun!' and I ducked. It *wasn't* lightning. Crouching, I ran back, trying to melt into the Charger's paint. Two more shots and I felt a tug at my left sleeve as I scrabbled to climb back into the driver's seat, slamming the door.

Staying low, I threw her in gear and prayed everything still worked as I floored the pedal against the red light. Her engine purred as she spun her wheels on the blacktop. Finding purchase at last, we took off. She growled, then roared as I hit over 60 mph on the side street, elated to be set free.

Stomach in my throat, I accelerated through the next intersection, barreling through oncoming traffic. I didn't dare brake, but one car did and skidded between me and the pursuing SUV, but not before a bullet shattered my back window. Another bullet hit the trunk, and I saw the muzzle flashes strobe in the side mirror.

Objects may be closer than they appear. "Aw shit…" I croaked. Launching over the next intersection, I landed hard, sparks flying from the exhaust, but I kept the pedal floored.

With a sharp right turn, I took my foot off the gas to brake hard. Then slid through the first left, skidding and drifting in the rain. I had much more power but only a touch more maneuverability than the SUV. When they slid through the last turn, they were starting to lag, but still hanging on my tail. I drove hard through a straightaway with two green lights and slammed through the next hard left, snaking through two more rights.

"Where the fuck *am* I?" I shrieked at the windshield.

Unfamiliar territory.

My demon-fueled car sped while I fought to get my voice in a recognizable octave, a necessary step to use the hands-free system for calling 911. After three desperate attempts, it finally rang.

I tapped the brake to take a wide left, then an immediate right. Not seeing the SUV, I veered wide and into a hard right through the open gate of an unlit home, almost bottoming out on the grade change as I flew in. Breaking hard, I slid a couple of feet to stop next to the house. Thankfully, the old concrete dampened the squeal. I threw Baby Blue in park, turned off the engine, then switched off the lights with the manual knob. I took my foot off the brake, so no lights would show, remembering every cat-and-mouse chase scene from every thriller I'd *ever* watched.

Peeking over my seat, watching for the SUV behind me, I waited on hold with 911.

"911, what's your emergency?" I jumped, startled by the voice.

"Someone's shooting at me! They hit my car at the light, and then they were shooting! *At me*!" I rattled on. "Like what the actual fuck?" I muttered to myself, waiting for their experience, wisdom, and assurances that they would stop this bizarre situation *instantly*.

"Are you injured?"

"No… I don't think so," I answered, still breathless.

"Are you safe, now?"

"Uh, maybe? I don't see them."

"Are you still inside the vehicle?"

"Yeah."

"Good, please stay inside and wait for units to arrive."

Then the operator started asking about where I was, who was driving, what kind of cars—the usual stuff. He had a calming voice that was somehow so soothing it felt nonchalant. Offensive to my ears, it sounded like he didn't give a shit, making it hard to focus and give him the information he sought. You'd think he worked at a government entity that didn't deal with life and death... like the DMV on a Monday.

For God's sake, give me someone who has the proper sense of urgency for this fucking situation! I screamed silently.

I wasn't really sure where I was, but I gave him what information I had.

Feeling suffocated, I went to slide the wet hood of my jacket down.

"Huh? What the... "I paused with my finger poking through the hood of my jacket. I was looking in the mirror, and even in the dim light from the windows of the house next door, I could see the hole. There was a bullet hole in the jacket's hood. *My* hood.

The one that was just on my fucking head!

"Oh my God..."

"Sir?"

In my panic, I ignored him and inspected my head in the rearview mirror. No blood.

It must have missed by a millimeter!

With my arms up, I became aware of a strange sensation.

I reached over, and I felt the wetness on my left arm. It felt thick and warm. Blood flowed to my elbow from a new hole in the jacket sleeve that I could see now that my eyes adjusted to the dark. *One* bullet hadn't missed.

My stomach lurched. "Oh my God. Oh my God. Oh. My. *God*! I've been *shot*! Holy shit!"

"We have an ambulance on the way, sir. Please stay calm." His statement carried *zero* excitement. No tension. No fanfare.

Who is *this guy?! Ignore his "No fucks given" attitude, dammit. Breathe. Just breathe.*

"Uh, okay… but how will you find me?" I asked.

"You gave us the main streets, and we have triangulated your cell signal, so keep an eye out for the lights and sirens and let me know when they're close, and we will guide them straight to you."

"Kay…" I muttered, willing it to be that simple.

"Sir, while we wait, can you think of any reason someone would want to harm you? To shoot at you?"

"What? I have no idea! Probably… random, I guess?" I replied automatically. *No one believes that anyone wants them dead, right? I'm a decent person. Nothing nefarious in my past.*

"Well, like… I recently found out I'm coming into some money—But that's crazy!" I mumbled aloud. A whirlwind of thoughts came unbidden.

"Sir, I couldn't quite catch that. Could you repeat it?"

Inheriting millions of dollars along with controlling shares in a large company because my uncle, who barely knew I existed, died and didn't leave kids. *That was pretty new.* My dad died young, too, so it all came to me; the only living heir.

So yeah, I guess that could be a motive. A reason. 200 million reasons, when you think about it.

I remembered my mother once said people will always try

to take anything you have that's worth having. A successful company and a fortune are something that most anyone would consider worth having.

The hair on the back of my neck stood up. I stared at my terrified eyes in the mirror as a foreboding filled me.

Other maxims intruded, like how you've got to spend money to make money, and something about breaking eggs for omelets. Collateral damages in takeovers. I don't know why the old adages popped in, but I helplessly followed the train of thought.

If I'm dead, someone else gets the money. People can find anyone now, especially with all the tech out there. They can pay to have someone found. Pay to have them killed! "Invest" to influence the outcome of money changing hands…

Shit… I'm the fucking eggs.

My breath came quick as my eyes darted from mirror to mirror, and looking over the seat for flashing lights. My ears strained to hear sirens. I had to calm myself, so I focused on my lucky rabbit's foot.

It's good, it's over. I'm safe for now; the shooters don't know where I am. The police are coming, and they do *know where I am. They will be here soon. They used my phone sig….*

"Oh, fuck."

Anyone can track a phone. Anyone with an investment in the right people with the right tools.

Always having lived the ramen noodle lifestyle, this inheritance seemed like a dream come true, a *gift*. Now I wondered if it was a wish gone wrong; a punishment for wanting anything at all. For being… greedy.

"Sir?"

But I'm not greedy… am I? I didn't ask for this kind of money. I already planned on giving a bunch to charity! Oh man, will I be like those poor lottery winners who were cursed?? Will I ever know any peace?! I asked the rabbit's foot as if it had the answers.

Hell, they can track the damn car, too! It's not in my name, but it wouldn't take long.

I remembered the mirror I broke the day before the lawyers called to tell me about my uncle. A bad omen. I played it off, but I should have known. All I wanted in life was the girl, a few extra dollars, and maybe the car. But now the last two felt tainted—hexed.

I don't need this! I don't ask to be part of this fucking omelet! I can go back… renounce the inheritance before they try again. Shove this wish I never made right back up the genie's ass! With any ounce of luck, my lovely date will be equally patient about all this, too. I mean… to be fair, I was shot.

"Sir? Have the units found you? Sir?... *Sir*? Are you alright? Just hang in there! We have units on the way!"

Oh sure, now *there's a little urgency in his voice.* His voice carried out into the night, and like the faint sound of sirens, it followed me as I skulked away with my hood pulled back up, disappearing into the wet darkness.

I left it *all,* with the phone on the passenger's seat and the rabbit's foot in my pocket.

Leah L. Churchville As a married mother of three children and two grandchildren, Leah worked in several fields, eventually realizing that none brought her joy like expressing her creative side.

She never met a glue gun or rhinestone she didn't like, and enjoys decorating, event planning, sewing, and writing. Originally, writing short prose and poetry for her own enjoyment, she has since decided to try her hand at writing short stories and novels. Encouraged by family, friends, and the Sin City Writers, she hopes to publish her debut novel in 2026.

Your Beautiful Heart

Jazmyne Hendricks

Your eyes…so enchanting, so true
I lose myself wandering
In your blue glimmer gaze

Your kiss…so sensual and deep
I'd hang for eternity
On your warm, tender lips

Your arms…so devoted, so strong
I melt within the caress
Of your gentle embrace

Your smile…so alluring and sweet
I ache for the radiance
Of your soft, breathy laugh

Your heart...oh, your heart…so passionate, so full
I'm forever grateful you let me inside
Your beautiful heart

Jazmyne Hendricks revels as much in writing darkness as in romance. She has penned over seventy poems, ranging in topic from social injustice and trauma rage to love and erotica.

Currently, she's working on her debut manuscript, a dark trauma-survivor romance titled, *Reclaiming the Night*. When she's not tethered to a pen or laptop, she can be found enjoying the company of fellow local authors, traveling, or relaxing with her husband, kids and dog.

For updates on her writing progress, fun tid-bits of her life and other wacky brain gems, you can follow her Facebook or Instagram profiles at: JazmyneHendricks.author

Excerpt from

Last Prom Standing

R.H. Bird

"So, why did we have to come all the way to Everhard's?" Pablo asked.

Big Dune was a small town. Mr. Everhard had coached my little league team and was originally my first-grade teacher. Who wouldn't want a teacher named Mr. Everhard? It was hilarious.

He claimed it was an English name, and his relatives modified it from Eberherd when they immigrated here. Seriously, none of them went to middle school? Nobody thought to run the name change past a thirteen-year-old boy?

With his wife, Vicky, they ran a pharmacy by that name, which made it even worse. They could've said, "Come here kid. We'd like to switch Eberherd and make it Everhard. What do you think?"

As soon as the boy snickered, that should have been the end of it. And after the first Everhards got made fun of a million times, why stick with it? You're in America, you can change it to anything if you needed another stupid name. Boner, Cornfoot, even Cockburn was out there. Why cling to

Everhard?

"Steve Platis is working today," I said.

"And?" Pablo lifted his arms.

"And he told me he's at the register. I need to buy a box of rubbers, and I don't want to get them from some little old lady cashier."

"You're such a wimp. What are you afraid of now?"

I held out my cash. "How about I give you the money and you buy them for me?"

"Not a friggin' chance. Even at Everhards, it's way too embarrassing. But since I'm here as moral support, I will stand off to the side and watch. I might even yell out, 'Is this kid old enough to buy rubbers?'"

"Please don't." He was joking but my face flushed hot and feverish. I wiped my hands down my pant legs to dry them. I had never bought condoms before and honestly didn't know if there was an age limit, like with beer and cigarettes.

He walked into the store first. "You're such a baby."

The Everhard Pharmacy used to be the Wang Pharmacy. Imagine that. When Vicky Wang married Mr. Everhard, she changed the name of the store to his.

I wondered if she debated hyphenating her name. Actually, I hoped her parents had a long conversation with her about it. "We've worked hard to make the Wang as big as possible . If you must take your husband's name, stick it in the middle. *The Everhard-Wang Pharmacy* will keep the excitement going."

We had shopped here since I was a kid and I used to love it because they had video games up front. If my mom gave me a dollar's worth of quarters, I wouldn't bug her while she browsed.

I heard the bell ding and turned toward the front of the store, making eye contact with Steve. He nodded and gave me a thumbs up. Earlier in the day I told him what I needed.

His shift ran until 6:00 p.m.

"So, what have you been using for protection?" Pablo asked.

On the way over, I confided that Piper and I had our first time over the weekend. He'd already heard about it from three other people. So much for Myckal and Porco keeping a secret.

"Piper kept going over to Robyn's top dresser drawer. Apparently, she has a stash of condoms," I said.

"You mean hot Robyn has her own box of condoms?"

"I mean super-hot Robyn has a *king-size* box! They must have ordered them through the mail or something."

"When am I going to see this chick?" he asked. "She can't be as gorgeous as you claim." "Dude, you would not have believed her in that towel. Come up with me one weekend.

You'll see."

Pablo shrugged. "We'll plan a road trip soon. In the meantime, why not just keep using their rubbers?"

After wandering around a few seconds, we found the right aisle.

"I don't know. I kinda feel like a tool always copping one from Robyn. Plus, I'd like to be able to have sex with Piper someplace besides her dorm room. Like, maybe when she comes home from college."

Pablo shoved me in the shoulder. "I bet Dan's are too big for you anyway."

"Too small, maybe."

"Speaking of small. Here's a box of minis for you."

A stern-faced mother passed behind me. She saw us in front of the condoms and gave me the evil eye. Her daughter looked about five. A green sucker spilled out of the kid's mouth, tumbled down her fuzzy pink jacket, gathering frizz along the way and landed on the floor. She shrugged and took another one from her pocket. That wrapper hit the ground, too.

I pointed at her and mouthed, *pick that up*. The brat stuck her tongue out.

When they had safely turned the corner, I stared at the display and scrunched my face.

"There's so many different kinds. Latex, non-latex, extra thin. What do we do?"

"To tell you the truth, buddy, I have no idea."

"What do you mean you have no idea? You've had sex before, right?"

He glanced over his shoulder. "Whisper, you idiot. Yes, I've had sex. Once with Jessica and two times with Nicole DeMayo. *They* always brought condoms. So, no. I've never bought any, either."

"All right. This looks like a regular box. I'll just buy these."

Pablo handed me a much bigger box. "We're not going through this again. You need to buy a ton of them now."

"Good idea. But I feel like a freak going up to Steve with *just* a box of rubbers."

Pablo crinkled his eyelids together. "Let's pick out some other stuff. Like the rubbers are just one thing on your list."

I nodded. "That sounds right. What else should we get?"

Pablo chucked an empty handbasket to me. "Ooh, here's vaseline, put that in there. And let's get a porno mag, too."

Before I knew it, all three items landed in the basket. "Really? Condoms, vaseline, and a porno mag. What is this, Saturday night at your house?"

Neither of us had ever bought a girly magazine before. When we were fourteen, we were walking through the woods. We came across a blue tarp that looked like it had been buried for a long time. A couple of the ends poked up through the leaves. There must have been twenty magazines under there. We scooped them up, found a much better hiding place, and that became our supply.

Pablo glared. "Okay, screw you. What do you want to get?"

"I don't know. Let's walk up and down the aisles and pick out a few things."

"I'll put the Vaseline back but you're keeping the porno mag. Steve'll let you buy it.

That's my charge for driving you."

Flipping the magazine over, I hid the rubbers underneath. "Whatever."

Pablo pointed at me. "I have a thought. How about we buy a bunch of awkward stuff that looks like we're buying it for other people?"

"Like what?"

He cracked a smug grin and tossed me a pink box.

I held it up. "Menstrual cramps?"

"Exactly. Plus, we'll get some maxi-pads, wart medicine, yeast infection cream, lice shampoo, and some anti-fungal stuff. That'll be for you."

"You're a moron, do you know that? Why did I even bring you?"

"Um, because you're such a loser, you still don't have a car."

After putting the cramp medicine back, we spent ten minutes picking out more reasonable products. I grabbed a razor, toothbrush, shaving cream, travel toothpaste, deodorant, two cans of soda, two candy bars, baby powder, and mouthwash.

"That's all I can afford," I said. "There's one customer at the register. Let's hurry before someone else goes up there." As Steve rang in that guy's stuff, I kept peering over my shoulder. I didn't want that mom with her kid getting in line behind me. In fact, I didn't want anyone in line behind me. My foot tapped and I pulled on my shirt collar. The guy paid and walked away.

"What's up, man?" I said to Steve.

He grinned and looked around for his boss. "Did you get them?"

I used a soft voice. "Yeah, they're at the bottom of the basket." As cool and nonchalant as possible, I bit my bottom lip and passed it to him.

"Excellent. Nice job," he said. "Hey, Pablo."

"How's it going, Steve?" He stood just behind my left shoulder.

Steve gave us a double thumbs up and got to work. He flipped over the travel toothpaste, searching for the price tag, when my worst nightmare happened.

Mr. Everhard limped over with his aluminum cane and knee brace, and slapped him on the back. "Steve, I'll take over here. Vicky needs help with some of the inventory in the rear of the store. Give her a hand for me, will you?"

Steve's face turned white, and his eyes bulged. "Oh. Okay, sure. But I'm already halfway through this order. How about I finish it, first?"

"Nonsense. I've known Luca and Pablo since they were young lads. It'll give us a chance to catch up."

Steve shrugged and mouthed "sorry" as he walked away.

Not half as sorry as me.

With a cheery smile Mr. Everhard rang up the baby powder and deodorant. "How are you boys?" Only the toothbrush stood between me and impending doom.

"Hi Mr. Everhard," we chorused together. Pablo's voice sounded distant as if he had slid closer to the door. I was on my own and knew it.

"Actually, it's Deacon Everhard now." His smile widened as he keyed in the toothbrush.

Oh come on! I wanted to yell. Instead, I muttered, "Huh?" Things had begun moving too fast for me to process.

"Didn't your mother tell you? I saw her just the other day. I've been ordained a deacon at the Big Dune Baptist Church."

My toes curled in my sneakers. "Of course, you were."

He cocked his head. "How's that?"

"I mean, congratulations." I closed my eyes, fighting off a panic attack. I heard the magazine pages rustle and listened for the keys, typing it into the cash register. That sound never came. When I opened them, his lips pressed tight into a grimace, and he shook his head.

"If my math is correct, you're not old enough to buy this magazine, are you?"

My birthday was November fourth. The cutoff for school years in our district was November fifth. That made me the youngest kid in class every year. So, I'd only be turning seventeen soon. Pablo was eighteen already. I could claim it was his.

But when I spun around, he had slunk away—the jerk.

My chin dropped to my chest. "I didn't know how old you had to be."

The deacon huffed. "Eighteen, Luca. Care to show me your license or should I return this to the shelf?"

Time slowed to a crawl. Maybe, it stopped altogether. "You can return it."

He squinched his face. "I can't say that I'm not a little—Whoa! What is this now?

Prophylactics too, young man?"

My stomach cramped. Deacon Everhard ran into my mother all the time. He had the power to destroy my life.

He probably noticed the terror on my face and took mercy on me.

"I can't say that I approve of this behavior. But as your pharmacist I have to be satisfied that you're engaging in safe sex. Between the AIDS epidemic and unwanted pregnancies, I'm glad you're making appropriate decisions. But I am including a brochure on abstinence, too. I'll place that in your bag."

I swallowed. "Thank you. Mr. Everhard. I mean Deacon Everhard."

He exhaled. "And don't worry. I was young once, too. I won't share this with your parents. The veil of privacy between pharmacist and client extends to your transactions."

All I could do was nod. Thank goodness he wouldn't tell on me.

"What the fudge? There's no price tag on these. Did you notice how much the prophylactics cost?"

"I didn't." I placed my cash on the counter and took a step back. "But here, you can charge me whatever you want."

A little voice cried out behind me. "Why *can't* I have fake eyelashes?"

"Because I said so!"

The mother and daughter got in line. My stomach spasmed.

"Don't be silly. I would never overcharge you." He motioned to one of his employees.

"Marge, will you come over here, please."

She turned out to be a little old lady with gray curly hair and bad posture. She wore a hand-knit white sweater over her misbuttoned shirt. Her nametag read, Mrs. Flanagan.

The door dinged and two smokin' hot cheerleaders pranced in. They each wore a school jacket. Their short uniform skirts fell at the top of their tan legs.

"Faith. Hope. What are you guys doing here?" Naturally, Pablo would run into someone he knew, and it would have to be twins.

"Us," one of them said. I could never tell which was which. "We live in this part of town.

What are *you* doing here?"

He pointed at me. "I came with Luca. He's buying a box of condoms."

Glancing my way, they both giggled. Hopefully, they

assumed it was a joke.

My brain screamed, *Are you kidding me?* I nodded to them, and my ribs squeezed tighter.

He pressed the button to activate the public address system and spoke into the microphone. "Marge, can you put this magazine back? Then amble over to aisle five and get a price check on this box of condoms, please. Our optimistic young lad selected the jumbo quantity and I believe they're on sale."

"Luca," the other twin emphasized my name, and they walked to the rear of the store.

My face burned red.

Clutching the magazine with two fingers, Marge held it far away from her. Everyone could see it was a porno. She winced at the condoms like they were infested with yeast. Out of the corner of my eye, the mother pushed her daughter behind her body, shielding her from me. Marge's voice boomed across the store. "I can't find a price sticker on the rubbers,

Deacon! Do you mind coming here and giving me a hand?"

Sneaking over, Pablo whispered in my ear. "Did she just call them rubbers?"

From the side of my mouth, I hissed, "Shut up. This is a disaster." I heard the twins giggling.

"For Pete's sake," the deacon exclaimed.

Marge and Deacon Everhard bent over at the same time. "Steve, you didn't tag the condoms properly," he called to the rear.

Steve peeked around the corner. "Sure did. I put them on

the end." He saw Faith and Hope smiling and ducked away.

The deacon screamed, slipping on that little girl's candy. He momentarily lost his balance, then stiffly regained it—not before clunking heads with Marge.

She stumbled backwards into the condom display. Her arms splayed to the sides, and she landed on a shelf. It kept her from going down. Rubber boxes cascaded around her, as if she were trapped beneath a waterfall.

"Son of a bitch!" Marge yelled.

The sticky little girl cowered to the other side of her mom.

Pablo couldn't take it any longer. He staggered behind the sunglasses, laughing his ass off. I buried my face in my hands.

The only way this could have gone worse is if my mother walked in right now. The door opened and Myckal entered with her dad. She came right over, all smiles.

"What are you two shopping for?"

I wanted to throw up. "Please, don't ask."

R.H. Bird grew up in New York, worked on Wall Street, then Honolulu, and back to Manhattan. In 2003, he and his wife decided to raise their children in kid-friendly Las Vegas.

In 2009, he published and sold a financial textbook to brokerage firms. The boredom spurred his interest in creative writing, and a writing retreat led to his YA novel, *Promposal* and *Last Prom Standing* (The Wild Rose Press).

He still lives in Vegas with his college sweetheart, who happens to be his wife, and their three daughters. He volunteers at the local church bringing Holy Communion to the homebound and the prison ministry.

Death by Miss Adventure
Chapter 5

S.G. Tasz

I wake up to a delicate tapping sound, followed by something small and dense smacking me in the forehead.

"Hey!" I look up. Shiva is sitting on the sill of the narrow window above my headboard. She ruffles her feathers and stares at me derisively.

"Gimme a break. It was a long night." I stretch and reach for the item she dropped on me. It's a box, wrapped in brown paper and tied with a drawstring bow.

A job.

Inhaling one last breath of clean linen, I push myself up to sit. Shiva squawks and hops over to the knot of fabric wedged in the branches of my nightstand to roost. I'm so grateful she knows to warn me when she needs to go outside. God knows how you housebreak a crow.

I slide the narrow window shut, then return my attention to the box. Shaking it only results in a nondescript thump. I toss it onto the nightstand and head for the living room. Work can wait. Coffee comes first. I open my bedroom door and—

"Dammit!" I must have left the curtains open last night, because the sun glancing off the pool outside has flooded the room with searing light. My eyes throb, and I press my fingers into them to make them stop.

"Oh good, you're awake."

Holy shit, someone is in my house.

I freeze, my hands still jammed against my eyeballs. Are they here to rob me? Because unless there's major street value in boxes of old books and *Quantum Leap* DVDs, they are wasting their time.

"Miss Adina Venture?" The voice, amazingly chipper for such an early hour, comes from the dining room. Turning away from the front windows, I pry my watering eyes open. Next to the door that leads out to the shed, the curtains in front of the patio slider are pulled wide. In the wild expanse of pomegranate and olive trees that has overtaken the rear garden, someone has cleared a rough path from the road to the deck. A tall cocktail table sits in front of the slider, and standing next to that, barely taller than the table itself, is a man. The sunlight reflects off the light brown skin of his bald head, and a thick gray goatee spills from his chin to brush against his chest. A pair of pince-nez glasses balance on the bridge of his nose.

Not a robber. Not someone I know. And *not* someone who should be here.

"Who the hell are you?" I demand, my voice still raspy from sleep.

He winces. "Oh, dear! Where are my manners?" He pats himself down as if searching for a business card. He's impeccably dressed in a black suit and a black pinstripe vest. His black collared shirt is buttoned to the top, but he's not wearing a tie. Instead, three loops of silver chain drape across his chest, fastened to the lapels of his jacket by pins shaped like skeleton hands. The knobby fingers curl inward and up, as if grasping for his neck.

My breath sticks in my throat. "Inquisitor."

He stops his fumbling and meets my gaze with a warm smile. "Yes, we are. Moses Mendelsohn, at your service."

I frown. "We?"

His bushy eyebrows pinch over the pince nez. "Do I need to present my colleague? His reputation so often precedes him, you see..."

He sweeps his hand toward the living room and the figure wedged in one of my low armchairs. He has coiffed blond hair parted on the side, a strong, clean-shaven jaw, and the same black three-piece suit as his colleague, albeit in a much larger size. When he sees my eyes fall on him, he stands, clearing six feet by several inches.

My mouth goes dry. If his legendary stature hadn't given him a way, his collar would have. Where Mendelsohn's is silver, his is a deep, glossy red.

Of course, I know who he is. Everyone does. Everyone like me, at least. They whisper his name in the shadowy back rooms and dark corners where Ops and fringe elements of the Non-Operational public go to be among friends. For all the talk I've heard about him, the headline is always the same:

God help you if you ever have the misfortune of crossing his path.

And now, here he is. In my living room.

My brain hums with terror. I want to run into my room and slam the door. But I won't give either of them the satisfaction. Standing up straight, I pinch my brows together in pretend confusion. "Sorry—*who* are you?"

His gray eyes narrow as he buttons his jacket. "Chief Inquisitor Breitling."

I blink. He's British? Funny that no one ever mentioned that. Other than the accent, his voice is pretty much what I would expect: deep, condescending, and irritated. He knows I know who he is, and how *dare* I make him introduce himself.

Slipping his hands in his pockets, he gives me a once over. A bemused expression crosses his face. Glancing down, I see why: I'm still in my grimy, dirt-streaked sports bra and shorts from the night before. A flush warms my face. Having an Inquisitor in my house is bad enough. Being half-naked as well is a top-five worst nightmare. I ache to cross my arms and cover myself, but I resist. No way I'm going to show an Inquisitor weakness. Besides, it's his job to pass judgement, so let him judge away.

"Okay," I say. "Now that we're old pals, maybe you can tell me what the hell is going on?"

Mendelsohn grunts, his mouth twisting as if he's tasted something sour. He did that the last time I said "hell" too. I guess Inquisitors are just as righteous as the rumors make them out to be.

"We're here on behalf of the Prime," Breitling says. He sounds as casual as if he'd told me they'd just happened to be in the neighborhood.

Shit. An audience with the Prime means one of two things: either I've done something right, or catastrophically wrong.

For me, there's only one way that dial is going to swing.

"What does he want?"

"Your presence at the Summit."

"Regarding *what*?"

"The Prime has issued a directive *and* has sent two Inquisitors to make sure it's carried out. That is more than enough to compel your obedience." His gaze is severe but placid, and the subtle streaks of white at his temples reinforce his frosty demeanor. If he ever turns up at a poker table, he'll have all the other players shaking in their shoes.

Mendelsohn, on the other hand, gives everything away. Worry lines crease his forehead and he is blatantly avoiding my gaze. That's conflict, maybe even fear. This little errand isn't sitting well with him, which makes it sit doubly unwell with me.

Facing Breitling again, I finally allow myself to fold my arms over my chest—not in self-consciousness, but defiance. "If the Prime wants to talk to me so badly, tell him to come speak to me himself instead of sending a couple errand boys to fetch me."

Breitling closes the distance between us with incomprehensible speed. I'm of above average height for a woman, and yet the way he towers over me makes me feel like a scolded child.

"This isn't a negotiation, *Exspiracarius*." He rolls the word in his mouth like a lion savoring a mouthful of fresh meat. "You've been summoned, and you *will* appear."

My jaw drops. I've only heard that name a few times, tossed around those shadowy back rooms I like to frequent. When the night has grown old and the music gets soft, and everyone is warm from booze and good company and looking for a story to chill their bones, they talk about the Exspiracarius. They spin yarns about strange deaths that have happened to friends of friends outside their direct social circle. The killer without a face. The ghost assassin. Be careful about who you hurt, the stories caution, because if you do wrong, there will be no place to hide. The Exspiracarius will find you. It is the second scariest boogeyman in the Operational world.

The first, of course, is the man standing in front of me. And apparently, that man knows not only that the Exspiracarius is real, but who she is. There's nothing to stop him from exercising the full extent of his authority on me. I'm sure he's done it for far less egregious acts. Even so, I can feel my hands tremble as they curl into fists. What he knows about me isn't important. It doesn't mean he knows *me*, and it doesn't give him the right to call me *that*.

My arm jerks backward. I don't know if I intend to punch him—I'm no boxer, and even if I were, he's got me seriously outclassed. While I'm trying to decide, he raises his hand. I recoil, but not fast enough. His fingers brush the center of my forehead before flicking outward like a starburst. My fist goes limp, followed by the rest of my limbs, and all thoughts of resistance crumble.

"Wha...."

It's the only sound I can manage before my tongue goes as limp as everything else. As I lurch toward the living room, hoping to land on something soft, I hear Mendelsohn sigh in exasperation. "Honestly, Levi, was that necessary?"

I DON'T BLACK OUT. I'm numb and stupid, as if someone has doused my brain in formaldehyde. All noise and sensation disappears, and what I see comes in stuttering snapshots. The blue and white loops of the deep pile living room rug. The cut of Breitling's jaw from below, silhouetted against the sun and tree branches. The ceiling of a car darkened to near black by tinted windows. A huge hand closing my eyes.

Darkness, marred only by green and red blotches.

We drive for somewhere between fifteen minutes and a thousand years. Long enough to think he may have broken me for good. Then I catch the scent of something lush and floral. Rose. It's nice. I inhale again, and my hands itch and burn like I've just come in from the bitter cold. That's less nice.

"She's waking up." The first of Mendelsohn's words sound like they're coming from the other side of a tunnel, but the last ones are clear and close. I test my eyelids, and they open without hesitation.

I'm not in the car. I'm not even laying down. I'm seated in a luxurious leather armchair, barefoot but thankfully wearing a sweatshirt over my bra and shorts. In front of me is a massive desk, and on the other side sits a man sporting a pencil-thin mustache and a dark gray suit that would cost more than my car if I had one. Behind him is an image of blue sky and sand dunes that, after a moment, I realize is not a painting but a picture window.

"Miss Venture," he says with a thick Spanish accent. "My name is Alfonse Castillo. *Bienvenido al Orden*. The Order welcomes you."

"What the fuck…?" I slur, the words sticking on my dehydrated tongue.

"Show some respect." Breitling's voice rumbles behind me. "You're speaking to the Prime."

I turn my head to see him looming over the left side of my chair. Next to him, Mendelsohn is wiping his hands with a blue handkerchief. They seem at ease, as if kidnapping someone from their own home is a normal part of the job—which, for all I know, it is. I glower at both of them for a moment before returning my attention to the Prime. "How did you find me?"

Castillo dips his head. "My apologies for the aggressive approach. Once you hear what I have to say, I'm sure you'll understand." His voice is warm and velvety smooth, but the light brown eyes he surveys me with are as hard as bricks. He's not going to answer my question, and I'd do well not to ask again.

I suck in a breath as the word "trapped" floats into my head. They are not going to let me out of this until they've gotten what they want from me. What's my best move here? Beg for mercy? The thought is almost enough to make me cackle. Even if they hadn't dragged me here against my will, these are Inquisitors. I doubt their dictionary even has the word "mercy" in it.

So, what's the second-best move?

"Okay, I think I know what this is about." I press my hands onto the desk and flash Castillo my most placating-yet-self-possessed grin. "I'm not registered. But I promise you, I've got all the paperwork at home, and I'll be sending it in soon."

It's not a complete lie. I do have the paperwork. I've had it since I came to Vegas twelve years ago. All sixty-two pages of it, including the lineage forms that require three generations minimum on both sides. Since Dad left when I was three, I had decided to backburner the whole thing until I was in the mood to take a traipse down the broken-glass deathtrap that is Memory Lane. Of course, once I started my little enterprise, however, I'd abandoned the idea entirely.

Castillo waves his hand. "Your registration status is not at issue. Though, of course, we would welcome an Operator that has such a...distinct set of skills."

My teeth clamp onto my lower lip. So this *is* about that. "Okay, I get it. You disapprove of my occupation. I don't blame you. It can get downright nasty. But if it's fairness or justice you're worried about, you don't have to. I've got due diligence up the yang, I swear."

Mendelsohn chuckles nervously, as if he's unsure whether he should find my words amusing. Judging from the smile haunting Castillo's lips, he's probably in the clear. "Your business practices are not why I've summoned you either."

My eyebrows raise. "Really? I mean, that's great. But...*really*?"

He picks at a piece of lint on his sleeve. "Oh, I suspect that the Non-Operational authorities—or the NO police, as you probably call them—would have something to say about it, should they ever discover you. And of course, if there is a God to answer to, then answer you must someday. But as far as the Order is concerned, we do not make it a priority to micromanage every Operator's life choice."

I sigh. It's a relief, but a brief one. "Then why *am* I here?"

His face darkens. "As I'm sure my Inquisitors have told you, we have a situation."

I burst out laughing. "They've told me nothing. The two of them broke into my house, then Jolly Green here knocked me out."

"I see." Castillo frowns at Breitling. "Again, I apologize. This is not typically how we do things. But as you will see, there are extenuating circumstances." He places a hand on a blue folder sitting on the blotter in front of him. "Does the name Darius Canelo mean anything to you?"

"Not unless he's a boxer." I think for a second. "Or a Blowfish."

He arches an eyebrow at me, then glances at Breitling. "Joking?"

Breitling nods. "Yes, sir."

"Ah." Castillo returns his attention to me. "Mr. Canelo was a Reaper. One of our best, in fact."

I've heard that word bandied about in the shadowy back rooms too. In Order-speak, "Reaper" is code for beat cop. From what I can tell, most of their role is handing out citations for expired or inaccurate registration records. Not a high-risk job, and yet the ominous way Castillo said he *was* a Reaper makes me think this departure was neither planned nor peaceful. "What does he have to do with me?"

Castillo passes me the folder. Straining against the depth of the chair, I grab it and flip back the cover.

Dear God, I wish I hadn't. The first item in the folder is a photo of a body slumped in a chair with its head tipped over the backrest. The short, black hair and turquoise three-piece suit suggest it's a man, and the lithe frame suggests he was on the young side. Everything else, from his hairline to his chin, has been…the only word that comes to mind is "pulverized." Like he's gone ten rounds with a gorilla in iron boxing gloves. A grisly mass of flesh and bone fragments gapes from where his face once was, and his dapper shirt and vest are drenched in a bib of blood.

"Why would you show me this? Why—" Reality slams into my chest. I raise my eyes to Castillo. "You think I did it."

He sinks back into his chair. "No, Miss Venture. We know you did."

S.G. Tasz is a multi-award-winning fantasy novelist from Las Vegas, Nevada. In addition to her published novels, her work has appeared in anthologies for the Nevada Humanities and the Henderson Writers Group. When she's not working on her next book, she's running critique groups for the Sin City Writers, meeting readers at local signing events, or cheering on her favorite sports teams, the Vegas Golden Knights and the Green Bay Packers. For more information on her latest publications, visit www.sgtasz.com.

Note to the Reader

The following preview is drawn from my forthcoming novel, *Blood of Sand, Heart of Stone*. This dark fantasy tells of a young woman with an unknown past who becomes entangled with an ancient Egyptian bloodline whose legacy refuses to stay buried.

Blood of Sand, Heart of Stone

Chapter 2: Wake the Dead

Chris Battle

The walkways were lined with rows of flickering pumpkin-shaped luminaries. Scattered groups of costumed revelers made their way towards the picnic tent set up near the cemetery's ornate, gothic entrance.

An orchestra played a rousing version of Mussorgsky's *Night on Bald Mountain* in the distance on this warm Halloween evening.

Several small buses ferried guests to popular sites of famous deceased residents, with docents stationed at each mausoleum entrance.

In one grouping of four, two middle-aged men, dressed in identical plastic grim reaper costumes. The others were two, twenty-something guys in dark-colored street clothes, faces smudged with black grease paint. They walked together in silence, keeping to themselves.

One of the reapers turned to the men in streetwear. "Don't forget the alarm. We'll distract them in exactly thirty minutes." He popped the cheek of the taller of the two with an attention-getting slap. "Look at me when I talk." He spit on the ground. "You're brothers, right. You the oldest?" he asked.

Joey, the taller of the two young men, nodded.

"You full blood?"

"Half."

"Thought so. The good parts, I hope. Where's the rest of you from?"

"Somewhere else."

The older man stared at the young guy. "Smart ass. Get out of here!"

The two brothers left the costumed men, walking away fast. Joey kept his shoulders loose and his face blank, like he was just another bored kid at a Halloween event, but inside his ribs his heart was thumping with anger.

Ray Ray didn't say anything until they were far enough that the reapers couldn't hear. Then he muttered, "I hate those guys."

Joey nodded. "Me too."

They caught a mini tour bus headed to the southwest section of the cemetery. An elderly woman docent, dressed as Raggedy Ann, greeted them from the front of the bus. "Welcome. Take your seats and we'll be off."

The brothers settled into the back row.

"I hate that tough guy shit," Joey complained. "Needs to keep his hands off me."

"Head dog gets to piss where he wants," Ray Ray said.

"You should know that being the older bro."

Joey scowled. He didn't say that being the big brother didn't feel like power. It felt like responsibility.

The lady dressed as Raggedy Ann grabbed the mic. "Next stop. See the final resting place of the inventor of the safety pin. I can hardly keep it together. This exit."

A few people laughed politely. The bus jerked to a full stop. Several guests exited and headed up a small hill on their right toward a well-lit mausoleum. The docent kept talking, her voice annoyingly cheery.

The two brothers jumped down and waited until the bus took off, veering left towards the perimeter wall.

"Over here," Joey said. "By that yellow banner draped over the outside wall."

At the base of the wall on the cemetery side sat a tiny electric flatbed truck. A remote lay on the front seat. The bed was loaded with wrapping material, hand tools, a pole, and a hand truck.

Joey pulled the yellow banner down and left it on the ground. He swept his hand under the driver's side seat and removed a gun case. Inside was a .38 special. He checked it was loaded, then shoved it into his waistband, where it sat like a cold second spine.

"You ever shoot somebody?" Ray Ray asked, quiet.

"Get in."

Two minutes later they arrived at a granite, pyramid-shaped mausoleum off a backroad and parked behind some bushes.

"How's the time?" Ray Ray asked.

"Three minutes before they start bustin' things up."

Joey grabbed his brother's arm and motioned him to be quiet, pointing at a lit flashlight weaving among the trees.

Someone moved toward them, about three hundred feet away. He pulled Ray Ray down next to him behind a bush. His hand went to the gun. He pointed toward the sound headed their way, praying he wouldn't have to use the weapon and divide his life into a before-and-after.

The two brothers held their breath.

The deep-throated growl of a dog rumbled nearby. The flashlight beam swept the ground. Leaves crunched slowly. Professional.

Ray Ray's breathing hitched once, sharp.

The dog made a sound that wasn't a growl. Like it caught something interesting. The beam angled toward their direction. The German Shepherd's nails clicked on a stone. A low whine. The beam came closer.

Just then the static crackling of a walkie-talkie cut through the air.

"Attention. All security officers please report to the event tent at the front entrance immediately. Code 13. Repeat. Code 13. All officers to report now!"

A man's voice answered from somewhere nearby. "Station Four. Copy, Central."

The handler pulled the dog in close. "Heel," he commanded. The dog hesitated. It whined again. For one second Joey thought this would be the moment he earned a permanent nickname like *Joey Two-Shots*. But the handler gave the leash a sharp tug. "Heel."

The dog whimpered, then obeyed, trotting away with its head turned as if it knew exactly where Joey was and was being polite about it.

When the flashlight faded, Joey realized his jaw hurt from clenching.

"Okay." Joey said. "You disable the camera in that tree while I get the door open. We've got fifteen minutes max. Let's do this."

Lightning flashed across the sky, followed by thunder from miles away, then silence and a sudden darkness fell around them. The perfect summer evening changed in an instant.

Ray Ray craned his neck. "Storm's rolling in."

Joey glanced up at the pyramid shaped mausoleum. "Good," Joey said, halfheartedly, "rain makes people look the other way." He broke the wrought iron door lock open with the practiced efficiency of a man getting used to violence. The lock gave with a metallic groan like it was tired of standing firm.

"Brace yourself," Joey said. "My friend Mikey told me these places can smell like roadkill gone bad."

Once inside, the room was dark and damp. It smelled of stale air, old stone, and a faint spoiled sweetness like fruit left too long in a drawer.

Joey sniffed. "Not too bad," he said, as though doing an online restaurant review. "Let's work fast though."

Ray Ray turned on a flashlight, propped it against the door, and tilted it so the light shone into the space.

A wall on the left held two horizontal casket-sized drawers. Joey walked over and ran his hand across the cold marble, tracing the engraved names and life spans of the crypt's residents. The Egyptologist's name was long and fancy, and his wife's name sat beneath it like an afterthought, as if even in death she lingered in the land of *plus one*.

A tiny table and two chairs sat in the middle of the space, set for tea service: a porcelain pot, two delicate cups, a little plate that held something dried and dark that might once have been biscuits—except Joey couldn't imagine anyone bringing cookies into a tomb unless they were either grieving or insane.

Ray Ray pointed. "Now that is creepy."

"Maybe they liked tea."

"Maybe they liked pretending they weren't dead."

Lightning flashed again, highlighting stained-glass windows set into the back wall.

On the right side hung several small tapestries and paintings showing court scenes of some ancient pharaoh and his family. Underneath them was a mahogany display case filled with carved scarabs made of vibrant turquoise, red jasper, and deep blue lapis lazuli stone. The scarabs were arranged in neat little rows like candy in a box, but the longer Joey stared, the more he saw tiny differences—one chipped, one repaired, one with a crack filled in by something that looked like wax.

On the second shelf lay several gold picture frames containing small pieces of papyrus with faded symbols. Each frame had a little handwritten label beneath it, ink browned with age.

Ray Ray leaned in, close. "Can you read that?"

Joey squinted. The labels weren't typed. They were personal, obsessive.

Spell for safe passage."

Another: *"Do not disturb."*

Another: *"Her favorite."*

His stomach tightened a notch. The tomb suddenly felt like somebody's private apartment in which he felt unwelcome.

Next to the showcase stood a full-sized, anatomically shaped cedarwood coffin. The bottom portion was painted with a short strip of faded hieroglyphics and images of court life in neutral whites and shades of beige with occasional specks of original red and blue. The spread wings of the god of the dead, Osiris, covered most of the lower and midsection of the lid. Above that was the faded picture of a headdress, a beard, and arms crossed over the image's chest. The upper lid was the face and head. Two extra-large, deep black eyes, open wide, seemed to shine with life.

Ray Ray walked over and touched the center of one eyeball. "Catch those eyes," he said. "So real. These are made of shiny shells. Cool." He shifted his body to the right, then left. "Damn. The eyes are following me."

"Stop waving at it like it's gonna wave back," Joey said.

Ray Ray grinned. "You scared?"

Joey made a face. "I'm not scared. I'm… uncomfortable."

"That's scared with a suit jacket on."

Joey turned away so his brother wouldn't see how quickly he crossed himself. Not fully. Just a little. Like a man tapping wood.

Propped up behind the coffin, against the wall, stood a larger-than-life statue of light grey stone. A sturdy linked chain was wrapped around its body, making it tough to see it clearly. The stone base the statue rested on had a faint glowing crystal embedded on the front panel in the middle.

Ray Ray approached it, eyes bright. "What is this? An elf, a vampire, a gargoyle? It's got pointy ears. Could be any of those." He tapped the gemstone with a fingernail. "And how do 'ya' think they get this white stone in the base to glow for so long. Must run on batteries."

Joey watched Ray Ray's finger on the crystal and felt something prickle at the back of his neck. The light didn't flicker like electricity. It pulsed, sorta' like breathing.

"And what does the light do?" Ray Ray asked. "Some security device?"

Joey shook his head and came over. The chain clinked faintly, and the sound seemed too loud inside the tomb. Joey gripped the stone shoulder and pushed. "Geez," he muttered. "This is a heavy mother." He leaned and peered behind it. Wings, massive and folded tight, carved with ridges and grooves that looked like veins. Whoever sculpted it had put too much love into it. Too much detail. As if they'd been copying something they'd seen up close.

"Look at the giant wings," Joey said. "Good thing this guy ain't for real."

Ray Ray tilted his head. "This is what they want so bad? What did you say…as bar decoration in some killer Vegas lounge?"

That's what I heard. Up close, the statue's face was half hidden by chain, but he saw enough to feel a chill: the mouth wasn't snarling. It looked… patient. Like it was waiting for someone to make a mistake. "Why chain a statue?" Joey murmured, more to himself than Ray Ray.

Ray Ray shrugged. "You chain dogs and inmates.

"Yeah. But you chain things that can run away," Joey puzzled.

Ray Ray stared at him. "Joey."

Joey cleared his throat. "Just wrap it," he said, too sharply. "Less talking."

Ray Ray glanced around again, suddenly quieter. "I get the paintings and other weird Egyptian junk, and the coffin is cool, but why's someone paying so much for this dude?"

"Guess they like the way he looks." Joey said and felt the lie in his own mouth.

A gust of wind howled outside. The mausoleum door rattled. A great-horned owl hooted forlornly in the distance.

Ray Ray jumped. "Did you hear that?"

"Don't get spooked," Joey said, though his own pulse had started doing that fast, ugly thing. "You know how many dead people are buried around us now?"

"That's not helping," Ray Ray said. "But okay—how many?"

"All of them," he said, and forced a laugh. "Start grabbin' things. Now. I'm callin' the guys outside the gate. Telling 'em to bring their truck in slow, lights off in twenty."

"We're doin' this now, even with the storm outside?"

"It's only lightning," Joey said. "Don't go chicken on me."

Ray Ray's eyes narrowed. "You're the one who crossed yourself."

"If you tell anyone that," Joey jabbed a finger at him. "Either get working or give Mom a call and ask her where she put your balls. Maybe she'll run them out here."

Ray Ray flipped him off, then started taking the wall hangings down.

Joey went outside to the flatbed and grabbed the padding and tools, but even out there, the cemetery felt different now. The storm had changed the air. Lightning made the headstones look like horror movie snapshots. The trees looked like people standing still, listening.

He went back inside and found Ray Ray piling artifacts into a padded bin. "Careful with the papyrus."

"Why? It's just old paper."

Joey didn't say, *Because this tomb feels like somebody left the room and might come back.* He just said, "Because we're getting paid for undamaged, not dust."

They wrapped the statue tight, layering the tapestries like bandages. Joey cinched the final knot and stepped back.

The crystal embedded in the base flared—brief, bright, unmistakable.

Ray Ray froze. "Joey?"

The glow dimmed, returning to its faint, steady shimmer. "Electrical," Joey said immediately. "Storm. Static. Old wiring."

"There are no wires," Ray Ray said.

He shot him a look. "You wanna' finish this job or stand here chatting?"

Ray Ray swallowed. "Finish."

They tipped the statue onto the hand truck. The wheels protested. The weight shifted violently, forcing Joey to brace his foot. For half a second, he felt resistance. Not weight. Pressure. Like a shoulder rolling under cloth. Joey sucked in a breath through his teeth. "Don't stop."

"I didn't," Ray Ray said. They rolled it out.

Rain hit hard now, drumming on stone. The cemetery

lights flickered. Somewhere far off, a transformer popped.

At the wall, Joey threw the yellow banner back into place. "I'll help you up," he said. "Then you pull me over."

Ray Ray climbed first. Joey followed. As he landed, outside, there came a sound from the other side of the wall.

Not thunder.

Not wind.

A sharp metallic clink.

Chain.

Ray Ray's voice shook. "Joey!"

"Don't," Joey said. "Do not finish that sentence."

Another sound—slow, grinding. Stone sliding against stone.

Joey turned despite himself.

The yellow banner was pulled down from inside the wall. Just slightly. As if something inside had pulled it.

Then it stopped.

Silence.

Joey grabbed Ray Ray by the sleeve and dragged him away.

They didn't run. Running would have meant admitting something was chasing them.

"Just the storm," Joey said. "Just noise."

Ray Ray didn't answer.

Neither of them looked back.

Chris Battle has always written short stories since her Chicago childhood. After moving to NYC she acted in several off-off Broadway plays, and worked and wrote on the side. After marriage, her family moved to Tampa, Florida. Here several of her short screenplays were produced by a local film group. Having moved to Las Vegas with her husband in 2006, Chris keeps busy with family and personal writing, and as an active member of the Sin City Writers, Group, Henderson Writers Group, and is an associate of the Dramatists Guild. She also recently cofounded a Vegas playwright's group called PlaywrightsStagewerksLV.

Ilya, a magical creature known as a witch, ventures into a cavernous underground ruin and encounters the strange remnants of a long-gone human civilization.

Excerpt from a novel in progress

Lucy Couch

"These runes, they tell of the lords and ladies who owned this house of rock," Vidra said. The indigo glow of her aura touched at the lichen and moss partially concealing the etched symbols. She scraped the blade of her elk-bone dagger into the stone to better clear them. "See? Lord and Lady So-in-So, glorious and proud, fair of deeds and worms. Words, I mean." Vidra leaned close. "Deeds and words."

"How did you learn so many of the runes?" Ilya asked. He crouched near a still pool of water where small silvery fish darted and danced. Pushing aside the cowl of his cloak, he peered down at the spry little fish.

"Unlike you, little brother, my head is not full of wool." The older witch laughed and jumped down a broken set of steps. Ilya followed her.

Vidra was not his sister, in truth. She had come one summer to his wood with a shy, timid witch in hand, a true sister made the same. Their fine pale hair shone the color of rosy dawn and their eyes were blue as cloudless sky, identical in looks but wildly disparate in habit. Where Vidra was bold, Anka demurred. When Vidra laughed, Anka cried. Ilya loved them both as true sisters but loved Vidra best for her mischief.

Bright auras cast strange shadows over the silent ruins as Ilya descended deeper into the underground for this new mischief Vidra wanted to show him. Snaking white tendrils of rootstalk poked through the dark decay and gripped into the shaped rock of the old city. Ilya ran his hand along one such crumbling wall as they walked and felt the comforting call from deep within of a lively wildness. Even here, so far below, a sense of belonging persisted. These ruins were part of his wood, a thing to know him and be known.

"My mother taught me the runes." Vidra climbed up a jagged snarl of root and rock and then turned to offer Ilya her hand. He gripped tight and let her pull him up beside her. "My mother knew from her mother, and her mother before her, on and on until some clever witch figured it out or knew from the men and mages who made them."

Ilya lifted his arms for balance as they crossed along the collapsed remains of an old wall. "Do you remember her well, your mother?"

"Some and none. She left when we were young. She wanted to see for herself where the waters stretched forever until sky and sea become one. My father had told her of such a place."

"My mother left under the full moon while I slept," Ilya said. His mother had been quick to smile and fiercely proud.

He barely remembered her enough to love her, but he remembered her songs and the smell of her. She'd been spring blossoms and musky milk, old leather and a laugh like gentle rains. She'd traded her absence for her cloak, and the fine woolen fabric still smelled of her.

Vidra glanced over her shoulder at Ilya. "Witches make poor mothers at best. I don't want to be one. Anka does. She hopes you'll give her a child."

Ilya laughed. "She'd have better luck asking the shepherd men."

"She'd claw your eyes out for suggesting it." Vidra giggled and leapt up to catch the lip to a sagging tongue of mossy rock. Quick as a skink she found purchase and scrambled up to crouch there at the edge. "Give me your hand, little brother."

Chipped, broken columns flanked the outcrop. Up above, two rounded domes protruded like bulging eyes. Ilya tried to understand what the building must have looked like before the forest swallowed it to ruin and shadow. His gaze caught on the curling, intricate symbols half-buried beneath glistening slick moss and dripping groundwater. "There are wards here."

"They're harmless," said Vidra. "You're not scared, are you?"

Ilya had not been frightened even when he woke to find his mother gone from their shared bed of leaf and limb. Sad and lonely for a bit, yes, but not frightened. Nothing gave a witch fear in his own wood, and these strange underground realms were still part of his wood. Dark and mysterious as the ruins were, his witch eyes saw clearly. Ilya clasped hands with Vidra to join her inside the old temple.

Stone statues lurked in dark niches along the corridor, hunched blackened beasts with bristling fur and gleaming jet eyes. Wolfish but wrong, too angular and lean, unmistakably a creature known to Ilya only as a fearful legend. "These are jarl."

Vidra waved a hand in dismissal. "They are stone, little brother. Carved to have the look only. Jarl are as gone as the men and mages who made them."

She led the way to a rounded chamber with a shallow, sunken pool in the center of the room. Murky gray glow hovered as a thick fog over the empty basin. Vidra walked through the wispy edges, but Ilya hugged the wall to avoid it as he followed her.

"This way," said Vidra. She ducked under a broken lintel and took a series of steps that spiraled down into deeper darkness.

Ilya was not afraid, but he did feel worried. "Vidra," he whispered. Even that soft sound rang too loud in the ominous silence. He could not even hear the drip of water and scurry of small creatures, of bats and moles and skittering bugs. No encroaching white rootstalk broke the dark soil nor did moss cling to the carved stone, and Ilya felt no longer that he walked through a realm buried within his wood.

"It's only a ways further." Vidra skipped down the steps. "At the bottom, is where I found it. You'll want to see, little brother."

"But what is it?"

"It'll ruin the surprise if I tell." She laughed and sprang ahead to disappear through a doorway.

Ilya followed her down a long passageway even though he wished to leave. If he admitted to being afraid, Vidra would surely mock him. She might not share future secrets with him, and Ilya loved the secrets and mischief they shared.

The passage opened to a long series of sunken pools, each hoarding gray glow. The ceiling above flashed and gleamed with the swirl and flow of countless interwoven wards. Stationed as sentinels along the passageway were more dark-stone statues of jarl with their bushy tails, sleek fur, pointed ears, and wicked-sharp teeth. Fine hairs stood along his neck.

"This way!" Vidra called. Her long, pretty hair floated and danced as she darted through an arched opening. More wards woven even tighter and more complex coated the massive dome of ceiling without any moss or lichen to obscure them. Occupying near the full of the room sat a round glowing pit sunk into the floor.

Vidra came to a halt at the edge and peered down into the murky fog. "Come see, little brother. Come see."

He squinted at the shadowy form beneath the coalescent glow of magic. It was large, whatever sat on the bottom of the pool, but the basin to hold it larger still. A series of metal rungs provided possible access down the steeply sloped sides. The thickly gathered fog obscured if the rungs reached the bottom or petered out halfway.

Beside him, Vidra crouched with her weight resting easily on the balls of her feet. "What do you think it is?"

"I'm not sure." Sinking down beside her, Ilya leaned forward for a better look. "I can't see what it is."

Something so large that had clearly once been important and now lay buried deep in the heart of his wood should not remain secret, Ilya decided. That determination along with amply piqued curiosity drove him to stick his hand forward into the luminescent mass. A static shock tingled over his skin as Ilya grabbed hold of the dormant energy. The glow solidified under the curl of his fingers and took on a brilliant green sheen. He cast his hand up and the verdant light rushed upward as a geyser, emptying the sloped pit.

"Oh," breathed Vidra. "Look!"

Down below them sat a hunkering twist of metal, a mass of flat ribbons and jagged-edged circles all interconnected. Magical symbols and ancient runes pulsed as a heartbeat of green light that burst brighter, faster, as they watched. Ilya leaned further to better take in the eerily beautiful sight. Being able to see the thing in the pit did little to explain its purpose or function.

"Ilya."

The calm but desperate urgency in Vidra's voice drew his attention. He followed her gaze up to the great domed ceiling. Streaks of brilliance darted and flashed through the intricate weave of the wards. More and more of the green light disappeared into the rivers of carved stone. It flowed through the curving symbols and traced down the etched columns that lined the chamber.

Ilya's breath caught. A horrible dread overcame him. From the thing in the pit came a low, shuddering groan and a metal-on-metal rasp. Emerald rays shot forth.

Vidra jumped to her feet. Ilya joined her, grabbing for her arm as she stagged back. Together they hurried for the doorway to the cavernous hall. The ground trembled and thrashed beneath them. Behind them came louder, thundering rasps from the pit. Lightning bolts of green struck across the dome of wards with a cacophonous shriek.

The two witches spilled into the passageway. Up and down the wide stone hall twinkled a hundred black stars, watching. Toward the far end, three shadowy statues moved forward. Ilya froze.

"Run!" screamed Vidra. "Run!" She shoved at Ilya, forcing him into motion.

Up and up the cracked and twisting steps they ran. First Vidra fell, then Ilya, until they both bore skinned palms and bruised knees from scrambling out of the depths. Trifling little scrapes, but they dared not stop to heal away the aches.

At last, they burst like bile over the stony outcrop at the mouth of the temple into the brighter safety of the forest. A roost of birds nearby took flight, cawing in alarm for the sudden intrusion.

Ilya fell into the rocks and roots below. He twisted upright and saw Vidra crouching with shining orbs for eyes. In her fist she clutched her elk-bone dagger.

"Those were jarl," she said. "Jarl hunt witches. They'll hunt *you*."

Thick pinpricks of unease skipped along his spine. He started to reply, but then she lunged for him with the knife still in hand.

Ilya scrambled back over the twists of earth and wood, heart thudding. He yelped as she caught him. "No, Vidra!"

Her laugh was the sweet song of summer warmth. "My dear little brother. I've known thousands of beautiful sunrises and seen great pattern of the stars. You are a sapling, young and tender. The next thousand sunrises will be yours -- run, beloved." Her aura blazed an icy indigo, then bright platinum, and Ilya shielded his eyes from searing darkness as the knife descended.

Lucy Couch lives in a house full of books that she shares with her husband and their hamster. She is a voting member of the Organization for Transformative Works, survived Strikethrough, and has been a frequent contributor to the Hugo Award-Winning project Archive of Our Own since 2012 where her stories have amassed over one hundred thousand hits. Besides writing, she enjoys travel, video games, and attending the Sin City Writers Group.

Lucky Ducky

P.B. Ray

"I don't like her." Frack crosses his arms.

He is back. Interrupting my writing. Again.

"Okay, what don't you like about her?" I ask.

"She's too much. She's like all over the place. You know?"

Phew. I really do not need this. Not now.

"No, I don't know. I introduced her as your love interest because I thought she'd be a good match, eventually..."

"Eventually? Couldn't we start on page one with her being more than that?"

"Pretty sure this is my story Frack..." I say, pointing at my laptop.

"Hmmph." He turns his back on me and I'm more than a little frustrated.

"Okay, tell me what you would like. And don't say sexy and hot, you'll disappoint me to my core."

Frack faces me. Looking very serious.

"Make her a lawyer, one who likes pizza and the Winter Olympics. Former ice skater. Long black hair and she needs a favorite weapon."

"Umm, okay. Not bad." I'm going to humor him a little so

I can get back to work.

"And she has a problem with body odor…"

"Frack, that's a given. Your entire species has that problem…"

"No, not my species. No. Human. I want a human partner. Hey! Where are you going?"

I'm standing, slipping on my ballet flats.

"To get donuts. And coffee. I can tell this is going to be a long day."

I grab my keys and purse and practically run to my car. These insurrections are happening more often the deeper I get into the book. My friend Marie who helps me edit will be amused but honestly, it's a pain in the ass.

I get in my car, look in the rearview and there are a pair of eyes looking fiercely back at me.

"Frick, I can't. Not right now." I put my car in reverse and ease from the driveway.

"You're not turning me into a human, are you? Just because he wants some kind of kinky sex scenes?"

I check my mirror. She is looking upset, her face a contorted mass.

"What? No. He didn't say anything about kinky sex. He's afraid you're outshining him. Which you are. You came out of left field, and I've been doing my best to even things out, but I can't, because Frack can be such a tool…and no, you will not be made into a human."

I'd run from one only to be confronted with the other. In my car no less. They didn't usually make it out of the house. I need an appointment with my therapist.

"Can we talk about these names, while I'm here? I saw

your last book and the characters have real sounding names… Frick and Frack?"

I glance in the rearview as I'm changing lanes and see she looks concerned.

"Place holders. I couldn't decide on names, so those will be replaced later on. Anything else?"

Why do I encourage these conversations? What am I doing?

"Why should I love him? He's got such a bad attitude. He argues all the time."

"He doesn't like to argue, but he likes to win, so he's gotten good at arguing. It's a flaw. You have them too… and he doesn't argue all the time…"

I pull up to Lucky Ducky Donuts and stare through the front window of the shop. Inside, one of the owners is putting the pink boxes together. I look in the mirror and Frick is looking out the side window. No doubt working on her next barrage of ideas and words, trying to shame me into some corner or other in my writing. I hop out of the car and go inside the shop.

Daisy, the owner's granddaughter comes from the back and flops into a chair next to one of the tiny tables. She looks bored and unhappy. Basically, she looks like a teenager. She gives me a smile that is anything but teen angst. I've just left a buttload of angst in my car and at home. I sigh and go to the counter.

"Six chocolate glazed, 3 twists and 3 apple fritters please," I say. "Oh, and a large coffee with cream."

Mr. Soo smiles at me, picks out a pink box and begins filling it with my order. He makes my coffee and brings everything to the register with a smile that lights up my world every time. It is a real smile, a genuine smile. There are a dozen places I could go for donuts and coffee, but none of them have Mr. Soo or Mrs. Soo behind the counter. They'd helped me out the day I was falling into a pit. They were there for me during a nasty emotional meltdown the day my divorce was finalized. Their kindness buoyed me. I will be forever grateful.

I pay and then glance out the window to see if Frack is still in my backseat. She isn't. She's now in the front seat using the vanity mirror in the visor to apply lip gloss to her eyebrows. I sit down with my box and drink at the table next to Daisy.

I take a glazed twist out to have with my coffee. I can feel Daisy watching me.

"I like your shorts and tee shirt Daisy. They look comfortable and cute," I say.

Daisy looks down at her clothes as though she'd forgotten what she'd put on that day. I know better. That took at least twenty, maybe thirty minutes to decide on. Her hair is a masterpiece of cute but messy. A look I've tried and failed at repeatedly over the years.

"Thanks. Don't want to go home?" she asks, looking at me. I have eye contact. It startles me.

"Uh, something like that. I've hit a weird wall with my writing…"

Daisy tilts her head.

"Has that ever happened to you? You come up against something and you just don't know what to do next?" I ask.

She nods but keeps looking at me. I wonder, have I brushed my hair? I remember brushing my teeth. I touch my head lightly.

"Do I have bed head?" I ask her.

"Yes. But not in a good way…" she says.

I laugh. "No doubt. I'm not good with hair. Yours always looks so wonderful. I've never had the knack."

I look back at my car. Frick is sitting behind the wheel now. Not a good sign.

"I love doing hair. I do my friends too. Want me to do something with yours?" Daisy is looking hopeful.

"Sure. Yes please," I say, feeling a sense of desperation that has zero to do with the mess on my noggin. If Frack shows up in the car I would seriously consider walking home. There is no way I want to be inside my car with the two of them.

Daisy leaves for the back of the shop, and I try to look away from the car.

To take my mind off the book I take out my phone and scroll the local news.

Daisy returns with a kitty shaped backpack and starts unloading it on her table. Eventually she has what she needs. From the corner of my eye, I see stacks of things including hair bands and make-up items. The lash curler brings back memories of my high school bathroom at lunch, trying to master the art of looking more like my peers. It never worked.

Without a word Daisy begins brushing my hair with firm strokes. She takes her time getting the tangles out and finally sets the brush down and picks up the comb. I haven't had a haircut in over a year. There are few things I like less than sitting in that salon chair in front of a mirror looking at myself. Ugh.

"You need a trim," she says.

Feeling like both of us needed some freedom in the moment, I say, "You can do whatever you want Daisy. You want to cut it? Have at it. Enjoy yourself." I take a sip of coffee.

She spritzed my hair. Water scented like strawberries mists everywhere, including my face. It smells and feels heavenly.

"What is that?" I ask.

"Water," Daisy says.

"It smells like strawberries."

"I know," she says, sounding a little annoyed. Adults could be so slow and stupid. She isn't wrong. I felt all of that right next to the gnawing anxiety of my current dilemma.

"I love it," I says. I do too.

She begins sectioning off my hair and pinning it, in preparation for cutting. A family of three walks in and I smile at them. Mom, dad and a preteen boy who made a beeline for the counters filled with sweets.

"Hold still," Daisy commands.

I did my best. Clip, clip, comb. Comb, comb, clip. Now I was wishing for that dreaded mirror. Not to see myself, but to see Daisy. What's her expression? What do her movements look like? I halfway expect one of her grandparents to come and object to us turning the front of their shop into a salon. It doesn't happen.

She pushes my head down and spritzes some more strawberry water. More combing and clipping and then she pulls my head up, her fingers cool on my forehead. I reach for the purse hanging on the chair back, put it in my lap, and start digging for the old-fashioned large coin purse I keep my money and credit cards in.

"Hold still," Daisy commands again. I stop pilfering my purse.

With the trim finishes she begins styling. I'd no idea what she's doing, and again, I want to see her.

She stops and reaches inside her backpack and pulls out a small hand mirror.

"You read my mind," I say.

When I hold the mirror up, she is back at work, and I can barely believe my eyes. She is intense. Frowning in concentration, lips slightly pursed as she combs, she sections, then tugs and begins putting the first band in my hair. It turns into a little donut wound round and round. She secures it with a bobby pin. She repeats the process on the other side. Then she sections and pulls some hair to the front and begins cutting. Wispy bangs. This takes a while. The mirror in my lap, I run my fingers over the handle trying to hold my position while looking down hoping to see something. My cheeks are in the way.

When she finishes, I peer into the mirror. My hair is styled like an Asian anime character. For the first time in my life, I squeal in delight. Literally. It is so unexpected, and so much fun. How many forty-somethings get special treatment like this in a donut shop?

I jump up and hug her. When I pull back, there is a real smile on her face. She doesn't want to take my money, but I insist. I go to show her grandparents. We all laugh. It is a love fest. So much so, I don't want to look at my car.

Reality knocks and I answer. Time to head home and get back to work. Frick and Frack are both in the back seat. The situation doesn't seem so bad now. In my mind, a solution is brewing.

When I get into my vehicle, no one speaks, which makes me feel even better.

At home I sit in front of my computer. I delete the first three chapters and start over.

Alana had been a medic on her planet, but here on earth, in this parallel universe she was a make-up artist and hairdresser to the stars. She met Garth when her car broke down and she was towed to the nearest garage. This happened while on location doing make-up and hair for a young pop star shooting a video.

He'd been a high-ranking officer in the military on her home planet and here he was a mechanic in a garage in Lost Hills, California. Garth wasn't really her type, but he was a rare opportunity to get in touch with her roots and reminisce about home. She would find they had more in common than they knew, but that was months down the road.

I look up and they're gone. I won't hear from them again for weeks.

When they return, they share that they want to get married and have a child. Their fights are epic and often funny. They love one another. They make it work.

The day the book goes to press I celebrate with a visit to Lucky Ducky Donuts, where I share that I'd dedicated the book to Daisy and her grandparents and the shop.

Alana and Garth drink champagne in the backseat of my car.

PB Ray is a long-time reader and writer. She lives with her characters on the written page, often drawing them in her sketchbook and will have conversations with them over her morning coffee.

As a fan of new and old folk tales and fantasy fiction, that is where many of her stories land.

She lives with her energetic dog Walter in Henderson, Nevada in a slightly untidy home because writing, drawing, painting and sewing come first.

F*cking Autocorrect

S.G. Tasz

Kyle

10:07am

Hey!
Sorry that took so long.

What happened?

System crash. One of the new software engineers screwed up some punctuation or something and the whole app glitched out. We had to push an update and everyone needs to reinstall before they can access the Sphinx patch.
It's a damn atrocity.
How are you?

Lol I'm okay
Finished painting the spare bedroom
Waiting for the

landscaper now

The joys of homeownership.

Haha
I just hope he remembers
to take all his tools will
him this time Makes me
wistful for our little
crapbox apartment

OK Jane Eyre.

Shut up :p

<3

Any thoughts on dinner?

How about burial?

Huh?

Sorry I morgue burial.
I MORGUE BURIAL!
Ugh.
I. MEAN. BBQ.

Haha

I think the glitch did something
peculiar to my autocorrect
shrubbery.
SETTINGS.

I like autocorrect
shrubbery better
Would make my day
so much easier lol

It's not funny
The proboscis is more smitten
than we thumping.

Goddammit.

ROFL
Do you need to handle that?

Yeah let me kill you later.
CALL.

Christ I hope that's what you meant :P
TTYL love you

Love you too.

5:27pm

Hey
Ordering dinner
What do you want?

5:58pm

Hello?
HELLO?
I'm getting you the brisket

6:43pm

When are you coming home?
I swear to God if you don't answer me you'll be in the spare bedroom tonight

7:32pm

Hope you like paint fumes.

8:06pm

HELLO???

Hello.

Ugh finally!

Where the hell have you been?

Somewhere.

Else.

What?

Hello?

8:28pm

KYLE?

When are you coming home?

Soon.

WHAT? TIME?

8:47pm

Fuck you I'm going to bed.

9:07pm

I see you out there you know

I'm not angry okay

I was just worried

Quit stalling and

come to bed

As.

You.

Wish.

RC

3:46pm

hey bro

New phone who dis

your brother dumbass

LOL hey

you around this weekend

Nah man I'm camping
with Tia
Leaving in the morning

cool

Dude you play the new
Sphinx patch yet?

nah man too weird

Why?

cuz what that dude
who worked on it
did to his wife
you heard about that right

Shit that was this game?
Didn't know that
That explains the Easter
egg tho

?

There's a secret level
where you chase a woman
through the woods and
strangle her
Some sick assholes idea
of a joke I guess.

yeah except he
killed her in their
house and he didn't
strangle her

How then?

well I heard he
cut her head off
with a pair of
garden shears

Fuck

yeah but that
might be a rumor
could be he just
stabbed her

Either way that's some
never sated

???

Never sated
Nasty* Shit*
Fucking autocorrect

LOL

S.G. Tasz is a multi-award-winning fantasy novelist from Las Vegas, Nevada. In addition to her published novels, her work has appeared in anthologies for the Nevada Humanities and the Henderson Writers Group. When she's not working on her next book, she's running critique groups for the Sin City Writers, meeting readers at local signing events, or cheering on her favorite sports teams, the Vegas Golden Knights and the Green Bay Packers.

For more information on her latest publications, visit www.sgtasz.com.

The Bell Diary

Leah Kathy New

I couldn't believe my luck. Cryptic Shadows, the coolest and scariest haunted house in the whole city, had hired me as an actress. I'd be the dead bride in the last room of the haunt. And everyone knows the final rooms are the most terrifying. Jumping out and scaring the kids from school, even the popular ones? That had to be the best feeling ever. Cryptic Shadows operated out of the old Bell mansion on the bad side of town, a truly terrifying place. None of the kids knew what happened at the mansion outside of the Halloween season, but that felt like part of the fun! The lore!

Anyway, it was opening night, and I had just finished putting on my phantom bride makeup. I gave myself one last look in the dressing room mirror and grinned. The plaster sores, the fake oozing blood; I'd really outdone myself. My zombie contacts stung a bit, and I blinked until they felt more normal. Nice effect. At the interview for the gig, I lied and said I knew how to do horror makeup. Thank god for YouTube tutorials and Spirit Halloween.

"Places, people!" shouted Manny, the owner of the

haunt. "You look great, kid." He said that last part to me as he ran by, making me beam.

"You got this." I whispered to myself, suddenly nervous. The night ahead seemed daunting and long; I'd be nocturnal for the next few weekends due to this job.

My friend Cam had also been hired, but they were in another room. I found them and we exchanged a quick high five. They were in the room right before mine, the one with the really elaborate fake bonfire theme.

"Are you ready for this?" Cam asked. They were dressed like a vampire and looked the part. I feared being bit!

"I was born ready for this!" I threw my head back and cackled, before giving Cam a quick 'good luck' embrace and entering my room.

Besides me and my dead groom, the other big part of our room was The Bell Mirror, an original part of the mansion. Supposedly when you looked into it, you'd see spirits. I'd give it one thing- it was HUGE. And the glass didn't look normal, like my reflection looked a little fuzzy and distorted. Manny said it's because it's antique, but I thought it was probably just a funhouse mirror dressed up to look haunted.

Anyway, my dead groom, Zack, was nowhere to be found. There were only ten minutes until show time, so I really hoped he'd make it! I looked around the room and rubbed my hands up and down my arms to warm up. Seriously, it felt super icy in there. I found myself standing in front of the mirror, staring at my spooky yet blurred reflection. I stuck my tongue out. So did my mirror self. I didn't see any spirits. Not that I actually expected to, but my imagination enjoyed the anticipation of ... something. The lights were still on, but soon the room would be dark except for the glow of small fake candles spread throughout.

A hidden door to the right of the mirror was where Zack and I were supposed to hide and jump out and scare folks. We could choose between that door and a hideaway directly across from the mirror, so we could sneak up behind people looking into the mirror and terrify them with our gruesome reflections. So much fun! I couldn't wait.

Where the heck was Zack?

Annoyed, I let my eyes wander and I saw something in the lower corner of the mirror. Something like paper... I bent down and poked at it and suddenly heard a THUNK as a big book fell down from behind the glass. The cover had a lock and looked like an old diary. I picked it up; heavy. And dusty. I'd have to investigate later, as right at that moment Zack came in with a "Boo!" and we took our places behind the secret door, giving each other conspiratorial evil grins as the lights went out.

I HID THE DIARY until I got home that night, or actually early the next morning. It felt sinful to take it, but curiosity got the better of me. Had I found something actually old, like really old? Could it be from back when the Bells lived there, eons and eons ago? I imagined all the possible writers of the diary on my drive home. Between the mysterious diary and sleep deprivation, I had worked myself up to a truly manic state by the time I closed my bedroom door behind me.

I plopped the book down on the unmade bed and sat on my desk chair, allowing myself to spin around a couple of times before focusing on the book. Picked the lock easily with a straightened paper clip. My hands trembled in anticipation as I opened the cover.

Francine Bell – 1925 was inscribed inside the front cover. Bingo, bango! One of the O.G. Bells. How thrilling! I wondered who she was, how old she was when she wrote this, if we would be friends if alive at the same time. I turned the page.

And found nothing. I flipped through the whole book. Blank.

Well that was a whole lot of anticipation for a whole lot of nothing. I sighed, disappointed and defeated; I shoved the book back into my tote bag to return to the mansion the next night. Then I went to scrub my makeup off and get ready for bed.

THE NEXT MORNING, the book sat on my desk. Weird, I remembered putting it in my bag before bed… didn't I? I absentmindedly opened it to the first page, and to my surprise, there was writing on it. Who had been in my room?! The only other person who lived in the house was my mom, and she never even opened my door.

It's a shame about your blouse. And that was all it said. I flipped through the book again, but this single sentence appeared to be the only writing. What the hell? I closed it and brought it downstairs with me to confront Mom. I found her in the kitchen pouring a cup of coffee.

"Good morning, sweetie. Want a cup?"

I nodded.

She passed me the one she had just poured and grabbed another mug for herself. "How was your first big night? Was it super scary?"

"Mom, why did you come in my room last night and write in this book?" I set it down on the table. She looked confused.

"I have no idea what you're talking about. But ooooh, that's a pretty book. Prop from the haunted house?"

"Then who—" I accidentally bumped my hip into the table, spilling the coffee from my cup all over my t-shirt. "Crap." I bent down to start cleaning up after my clumsy self when I remembered the writing in the book. It knew that I would spill coffee all over myself? No effing way. I opened it again. Blank.

THAT NIGHT, AS I got ready for my second shift at the haunt, I pulled the book out again. Opened to page one.

Don't worry, the important thing is that everyone is okay, is what the diary now said on page one. I shrugged and put the tome back in the tote bag. This thing was going back where it came from.

On the way to work, I got into a little fender bender, just barely tapping the car ahead at a stop light. We peacefully exchanged information, and it felt like things were fine. Mom would kill me when she found out, but that was a problem for the tomorrow me. This must be what the damn diary meant. Spooky, and not in a fun way.

When I entered the Bell Mirror room that night, I found Zack already there. He had his groom outfit on, but tonight instead of makeup, he wore a creepy rubber zombie mask with bulging eyes. I looked in the mirror, straightening my veil.

"You sure that mask is the way to go?"

No answer.

"Okay, great job creeping me out. Really, bravo!" He remained mute, and went into the hidden space, closing the sliding door behind him. Nope, he could stay there by himself, the creeper. Screw that. I hid in the other spot, across from the mirror.

That night, we scared the crap out of tons of people. It would have been more fun if Zack had been his usual self, instead of the silent freak act he had going on. But the screams from the guests? Awesome. I had to admit; his mask? A freaking hit.

At eleven, there was a thirty-minute lunch break for the actors when the haunt closed down and the lights turned on. I took the opportunity to remove the diary from my bag in the dressing room, determined to put it back where I found it and to forget about the whole thing. When I got back to the room, Zack stood in front of the mirror, staring straight ahead, not moving. The mask's nose inches away from the glass. Disturbing.

"Zack?" No answer. "Zack, you're being really weird tonight. Take off the mask so we can talk. You're freaking me out."

He stood there for another minute, then his arms started to slowly move up, hands reaching for the side of the mask. Just then the book fell onto the floor and it spun open to the first page, which had writing again.

Don't let him take off his mask.

Leah Kathy New is a Las Vegas local who believes life is better with rescue chihuahuas—and she has two to prove it! A proud queer author, Leah spins contemporary LGBTQ+ tales full of heart, sass, and just enough tragedy to make you cry into your martini before laughing again. When she's not crafting novels about love and identity, she's conjuring YA spooky short stories that make readers sleep with the lights on. Fueled by Diet Coke and curiosity, Leah celebrates diversity, thrills, and the joy of finding yourself in unexpected places. Bonus points if there's a ghost involved.

Demon Core

(intro to larger story)

Ian Sweet Couch

The inside of the containment area was eerily undisturbed and inappropriate for its museum qualities, the way parents might keep their missing child's room untouched for decades, down to edge-torn comics on the dresser. The containment room used to be a working laboratory. One side still had desks with recipe of the day calendars, vacation photos pinned to a corkboard, stacks of dusty printouts. The other side had a glass dome which stood as high as Henry's shoulder and was wider than he was tall.

Henry tried to not look at the contents of the dome directly. It felt like staring into the sun. His peripheral vision allowed him to catch glimpses of an empty dot, featureless and beyond black, surrounded by a halo lit up like a welding arc. A small black hole.

Surrounding the dome, which contained the hovering pinprick through the universe, was a field of broken glass. The glass once belonged to a larger dome which had protected the remaining one.

"Look how tiny the shards are over here." Jessica squatted next to the dome and pointed to a patch of glass that sparkled like diamonds.

Elsewhere surrounding the dome, the glass had come down in chunks. Most of the pieces landed in a groove cut into the office carpet when the structure had been hastily sunk into a concrete seal.

"So that's where it was struck?" Henry asked. "Then the rest just shattered?"

Jessica sat far too close to the dome; she could have reached out and touched it without fully extending her elbow.

Then she did.

"Check this out," she said. She scratched at the glass surface of the remaining dome with her fingernail. "There's a chip missing. That means whoever broke the outer dome swung through with a hammer, or something, and nicked this one. I guess we got lucky." She kept scratching and Henry could hear her nail pop in and out of the missing chip.

"Stop it," Henry said. He tried to look at the pockmark while struggling his vision away from the black dot looming nearby.

Jessica withdrew her hand and shot Henry a defensive glance. "I seriously doubt this dome is even doing anything. Don't worry." She stood up and folded her arms.

"Just stop it," Henry repeated. He sighed, drawing in the stale air and feeling his sinuses crackle against the recently stirred dust. Tightness in his lungs told him a combination of nerves and dust threatened an asthma attack. Patting an empty jacket pocket, Henry remembered his spent inhaler and calmed himself as best he could with shallow breaths.

When he could breathe, Henry gave in and studied the dome's contents.

The light looping around the hole seared his vision, and Henry squinted and consciously fought the instinct to avert his eyes from the light.

Fighting the hole itself was different. The dark pin hole drew his gaze as if fishing line had pierced his corneas and tugged them ever forward. When he looked away, a burning ring encircling an endless emptiness imposed itself over the room.

Henry studied the chip Jessica has scratched at, and the vision of the hole followed. "There's plenty to worry about," he said. "Someone's trying to kill us."

The dome served to ensure the beast was not fed. Inside the remaining dome, the miniature black hole had created a vacuum years ago. Henry and the other folks still acting as guardians liked to think it starved the hole of air molecules. They normally kept the room dark so that photons were not added to the hole's mass, which would in turn only cause it to grow faster.

But there had been a third dome. When installing the first glass structure, the encasement had been slung too close to the hole and was consumed as fast as light. There then gone. The defensive barrier blinked to oblivion. A researcher whisked out of existence too. He still hung frozen in the searing bands of the black hole's corona, a fixed mote of red light eternally traversing the event horizon. In many physics models, he will fall into the hole and be torn apart atom from atom forever and ever.

Eventually, and as fast as light, the hole would cross a

mass threshold and blip into the size of a planetoid to consume the solar system. For somebody to destroy the outer dome, to chip the final barrier, was lunacy. Hurrying the death of all known life into a rushed suicide.

Henry focused on his breathing, which whistled deep in his throat. After a moment, he spared the air to speak. "We need to stop this." He kicked at a large piece of glass and sent it skittering past Jessica, who tracked the shard's progress across the floor. "We need to find out who's doing this and, you know, stop them." Fluorescent lights hummed above him and several flickered.

Jessica shrugged.

"You don't think we should?"

"Not that," she said, "I just don't think it matters. I mean, that dome probably isn't doing anything. If you broke it right now, it'd probably make a loud *bang*!" Jessica clapped her hands, "because of the all the suction, then nothing. Maybe some of the glass would get absorbed? I dunno."

"The dome is at least slowing the hole down," Henry said.

"Right, maybe. Or the hole is just drawing molecules off the concrete below, or it'll create such a big vacuum that, when the hole eventually overcomes the dome, the collapse will implode the whole building. Even if that dome holds off rapid expansion for a couple of years, so what?"

Henry waved his hands, cutting her off. "Get out then, I need to stop-" He shooed her toward the exit. "Leave so I can turn the lights back off."

Jessica sighed, but she didn't seem to mind the dust. Henry followed her out while remembering to flip off the dying fluorescents.

OUTSIDE, THE SUNSHINE cut through the cold air so that Henry felt warmth on his skin and a chill beneath his jacket. Winter in the desert.

"We'll start with Bradley," said Henry. He pointed to a guard station across a small parking lot and down a quarter mile of gravel road. The station stood sentry at the edge of the facility grounds, next to a chain link fence topped with cycloned barbed wire and a gate with a snapped lowering bar.

"Give it a minute," said Jessica. She pulled a pack of cigarettes from her coat and shook one out. The cigarette adhered to her lip, dangling while she applied a jet butane lighter. Jessica dragged deep, held her breath, and shook the lighter. Frowning at whatever the shaking told her, she chucked the lighter into an empty patch of neglected desert scrub beyond the parking lot. Jessica exhaled a white lungful of smoke.

"Are you ready now?" asked Henry. He crinkled his nose at the smell and again felt his lungs tighten.

"Let me smoke. It's been a long day and it's going to get longer, so give me seven minutes."

In the distance, one of the physicists who had not produced new data for nearly a year stumbled down the front steps of his trailer and spit into the dirt. Drunk. His open bathrobe revealed a stained T-shirt with a kid's cereal mascot and a baggy pair of sweatpants. He stumbled in a circle before facing away to lean his forehead against the chromed siding next to his front door. After the man fumbled at his waistline, Henry realized he was urinating. The physicist finished, waved to Henry, and returned inside.

Henry rubbed his arms against the cold. "Who do you think did it?"

"The dome? Anybody. There's no telling. Anyone left here is crazy, and crazy people do crazy things." Jessica exhaled another plume which drifted in Henry's direction.

He fanned his hand in front of his face and scowled.

"Sorry," Jessica said. She took another drag and blew away against the wind. "What do you think happens in the black hole?"

"Nobody knows that." Henry flexed his fingers.

"I've told you. It's tidal forces and spaghettification. We either get mulched or frozen in time dilation. Probably both. The hole scrubs consciousness. It's nothingness."

"It doesn't have to work like that. You don't know."

Jessica broadcast incredulity. "Yes, I do. Depending on how bad the time dilation really gets, according to theory, we might *already* be dead." She hissed a laugh through her teeth and shook her head.

"Anyway." Henry toed gravel into a divot. "When I shouted for everyone this morning, Bradley was the first out of his house. He was already in his uniform, so who knows how long he'd been up. Maybe he has an idea who broke the dome."

"I saw him, too. I wondered why he was already awake," said Jessica.

"I wonder why nobody but you and me stayed awake after the news."

"Because nobody cares like you do, Henry." Jessica took another drag off her cigarette. The cherry glowed as she inhaled.

"So why do you care?" he asked.

She coughed and let out a gust of smoke.

Henry felt the vice clamp back on his chest and dodged away from the smoke. He fought against joining Jessica's coughing fit and lost. Closing his eye, Henry focused on the whistle piping through his throat.

"Oh my God, are you okay?" Jessica exclaimed. She glanced between Henry and the cigarette suspended between her fingers, threw down the cigarette, and ground it into the gravel beneath her boot. "I'm so sorry."

Henry patted down the air between himself and Jessica, indicating he would recover. His breathing became deliberate, working towards a steady trickle of oxygen.

"Where's your inhaler?" Jessica asked while looking around, as if it had been waiting outside the laboratory for them.

"It ran out." Henry timed his breaths for a response. "I have more. In my office."

"Shouldn't we get one?"

Henry shook his head. The whistle had left and the trickle of air became a rivulet. "After talking to Bradley. Easy on the smoking until then." He allowed himself the luxury of a pinched sigh. "Let's go," he said, already crunching up the gravel drive towards Bradley's guardhouse.

{The investigation continues in the complete work}

Ian Sweet Couch wrote for a sketch comedy show for five years, headed ad development at a small-town television studio, earned his MFA in Fiction, and has achieved a smattering of short story publications. He currently lives with his family in Las Vegas and is writing his third book.

Something He's Always Wanted

Terri Maue

Harold was starting to get annoyed by the time the angel arrived, because it was clear to him that he'd been dead for some time. Heart attack right there in the hardware store during inventory. He'd floated up out of his body, watched Arnold and Jason rush over, alarmed by the clatter of falling one-pound nails, saw them do the CPR routine, knew it was over.

After that, well, just formless nothingness. It was pleasant, but how long does a guy have to wait? You'd think things would be more organized. Then he felt a soft, light touch on his shoulder and there the angel was, hovering by his side.

"Time to go." She took his hand in hers, a gossamer thing, and they floated off.

"Where are we going?" Harold asked.

She smiled beatifically. "I'm taking you to your reward."

Death Notice:

HANDY Harold G. W., beloved husband of Rose, devoted father of

> Frederick (Marsha) and Sharon, dear brother of Anita (Robert) Ocster, loving grandfather of Timothy and Carol. March 27, 2006. Age 62. Owner of Handy's Hardware in East Sweetwater, holder of a patent for polymer saw blade coating, regular contributor to *Hardware World*, 30 year member of the Shriners, veteran of the United States Marine Corps with service in Vietnam. Funeral Tuesday, March 31, 10 a.m. at Chapel of God, 1217 Blackberry St. Friends may call at 9 a.m. Memorials to Young Entrepreneurs of Sweetwater.

"Well, your brother certainly would have liked that obituary," remarked Bob Ocster.

"He should." Anita folded the paper in her lap. "He wrote it."

"What?"

Anita laughed tightly. "Every word, my dear. And he made poor Rose promise to put it in the paper exactly as written, along with that ridiculous photo of him in the Shriner's hat."

"Well, damn. Still ruling, even from the grave."

"Actually," said Anita, "according to Rose, he planned his entire funeral, almost obsessed about it. 'I want you to celebrate my life,' he told her. 'Don't cry for me.' Then he'd say that the only thing that kept it from being perfect was that he wasn't going to be there to enjoy it."

"So like him." Expertly Bob rotated the Cadillac's steering wheel with one hand, using the heel of his palm to make the 90-degree turn into the parking lot.

Anita surveyed the lot. "Doesn't look like there are very many people here. Let's wait in the car for a few minutes."

On the lower level of the chapel, in a room most often used for Bible study and teen dances, Harold Handy lay in his coffin. Illumined by soft reflected light, he looked almost dapper in a charcoal suit, crisp white shirt, and neatly knotted red tie. His Shriner's fez was tucked beside his right elbow.

In a far corner, as distant as one could get from the coffin, the new widow and her daughter Sharon held cups of untouched coffee.

"Thank God, it's over," said Rose. "It's over and I'm free at last."

"Mom!" Sharon's whisper was fierce. "Please. What would people think if they heard you talk like that?"

"I really don't care." Rose slapped the cup down on the plastic tablecloth. The coffee splashed. She ignored it. "Thirty-four years I put up with him. Thirty-four years of dinner on the table precisely at five. Thirty-four years of 'not too much starch in the shirts or you do them over, missy.' Thirty-four years of, 'Here's your grocery money, now spend it carefully.' Like I was a child! Or worse. I could barely breathe."

Sharon patted her mother's arm. "I know, Mom. He wasn't easy to live with."

"Damn right!" Rose brushed off her daughter's hand. "But I'm going to have a good time with his money now; serves him right." She fixed Sharon with a quizzical look. "I don't know why you're all of a sudden defending him. It wasn't like he was a terrific father to you."

Reddening, Sharon dropped her gaze. "Yeah, I know. My psychiatrist has been encouraging me to face my 'father issues.'" She raised her eyes to her mother. "Do you really think Patrick and I would have been happy?" Her voice cracked.

Rose stifled a snort and laid her hand on her daughter's shoulder. "It was cruel what your father did. Bullying the poor young man until he couldn't take it anymore … and for what? Just because Harold always had to be the one in charge."

She hugged Sharon to her, trying to soothe her daughter's ragged breathing. "He's gone now. You have the rest of your life free of him. I'm sure you'll find happiness."

"I do hate him, Mom," Sharon murmured. "God help me, but I do hate him."

"I know. I hate him, too."

Across the room, Fred and Marsha appeared in the doorway with their three-year-old twins. Marsha gripped a small hand in each of hers, pulling tightly so that the children were forced to walk rigidly by her side. Fred trailed behind her, fiddling with his pipe, looking around for an ash tray into which he could knock the spent tobacco.

"Timothy and Carolyn," Marsha said sternly. "Remember your manners." Timothy squirmed, but she held him firmly. "We need to go over and pay our respects to grandpa and then go see grandma."

She shot a look at Fred, who was still casting about for a

place to dispose of his pipe ashes. "Frederick, you might give me some help with these two."

Fred ignored her for another moment and then shoved his pipe, still full of burnt tobacco, into his jacket pocket. Marsha grimaced, glaring pointedly at the bulge, but Fred forestalled any comment by taking charge of Timothy. "Come on, Tim. Let's go pay our respects to dear grandfather."

Marsha smoothed her pencil slim skirt and brought her lips close to Fred's ear. "You needn't take that attitude in front of the children."

Fred swore he could feel ice forming in his ear canal.

"I know perfectly well how you feel about your father," she went on, "but after all, he is—was—their grandfather and they loved him." Turning on a stiletto heel, she dragged Carolyn toward the coffin.

Fred sighed, and Timothy lifted his moon face toward him. "You mustn't blame her," he said softly to his son. "She's miserable because I'm miserable. And I'm miserable because I didn't have enough spine to resist Dad."

He let Timothy pull his hand free and squat down to look at something on the floor. "You'd think after all these years, I'd be over it." Fred spoke to the top of his son's carefully combed, slicked back hair. "See, Tim, I wanted to be an archeologist, but Dad wouldn't have it. 'No money in that, boy,' he said. 'Digging in the dirt—what kind of job is that for a man? No sir! No college money for that.' As if counting screws and bolts and singing the praises of septic tank cleaners was some kind of noble, manly occupation.'"

Timothy closed pudgy fingers around a crumpled door prize ticket.

"And I," Fred swallowed hard, "I just crumbled under his relentless badgering. Went to school, got a 'regular' job, got a wife, got a mortgage, got you kids ...." He shot a look toward the coffin, where Marsha had lifted Carolyn so that the little girl could peer in. "I hate my life," he muttered. "I'd almost rather be in there with Dad. Hell, I feel like I've been nailed in a coffin all my life; I might as well be dead.

Leaving Timothy to play on the floor, he wandered across the room in the general direction of the coffee urn. As he passed among the sparse gathering, he hardly noticed the comments and snatches of conversation in the air.

"He looks terrible," said Ruth, the neighbor across the street from the Handys.

"Well, if you mean all fake-like, I agree," said Alice. "He looks like he did when he was going to one of his important meetings."

Ruth snorted. "Yeah, Mr. High Poobah or something. I noticed he was too good to take out the garbage; his wife had to do that."

"Yeah, well, he was king of his castle," said Alice.

A FEW FEET AWAY from the two women, Ralph, a fifty-ish man, ran a hand over his balding head. "At least we won't have to see any more of those awful, tedious articles in *Hardware World,*" he said. "I never could figure out why they published that stuff of his."

"Maybe he caught the editor doing something unmentionable with a socket wrench." His companion punched Ralph on the arm and laughed.

LEANING AGAINST a wall in the windowless room, Jason and Arnold conversed in low voices. "If I had to hear one more story about his precious saw blade coating, I was going to be tempted to use the damn blade on myself." Jason rubbed a gangly hand over his sparse, teenage beard.

"Yeah, me too," said Arnold. "But what really drove me crazy was having to hear over and over how his name was perfect for the name of the hardware store."

Jason tugged nervously at the shirt sleeve cuff of his ill-fitting suit. "Did you really try to save him?" he asked.

"Well." Arnold pushed up his glasses. "I never was much good at CPR. But I gave it my best shot."

"I couldn't help thinking how funny he looked, sprawled there with nails all around him," said Jason.

Arnold scoffed. "I couldn't help thinking how when he came to, the first thing he'd probably do is yell at us for the big mess."

AT THE DOORWAY, Julie poked her head into the room. With a rush of relief, she hissed toward her friend. "Angie." Julie hurried toward her. "What are you doing here?"

"Same as you, I bet." Angie screwed her freckled face into a frown.

"Your mom made you come?"

"She said somebody had to represent the Young Entrepreneurs, and since I was president, it should be me."

Tugging at her curls, Julie huffed. "I bet they called each

other. That's practically the same thing my mom said to me, except I'm vice-president."

They turned together and looked toward the coffin. "Bet your mom didn't know anything about how he treated us," Angie muttered.

"The creep."

A BARREL-CHESTED man pushed a wheelchair toward the coffee table. "You know, George, we shouldn't be here."

"Why not?"

"The obit said 'friends' may call. We're not friends."

"Not *his* friends anyway. But his family might feel better just to see people here."

"Yeah, that's true. Not their fault they had to live with that self-centered blowhard."

Harold Handy flew in weightless joy alongside the beautiful angel. "My reward?" he said. "What is it?"

"Ah," said the angel, "it's something you've always wanted."

"Something I've always wanted ..."

At that moment, Harold looked down. He and the angel were hovering above the Chapel of God. In the lower level of the building, he saw his body, lying in resplendent repose in the magnificent coffin he'd selected. He raised shining eyes to the angel.

"Yes," said the angel. "You're going to get to be there for your own funeral, starting right this moment."

"Oh boy!" said Harold, as they floated through the walls

and settled near the ceiling above the casket. "I can hear them talking! This is going to be great!"

Terri Maue is a retired English professor, now pursuing her dream to write mystery novels. Her first novel, *Knife Edge,* was published in 2023 by Camel Press. The second, *Dark Mirror,* was released in January 2026. The series features a satirical columnist who yearns to write investigative journalism, her smokin' hot crime-reporter lover, and her highly intuitive—but don't call her psychic— lifelong friend. Terri is a proud member of Sin City Writers. She has dedicated *Dark Mirror* to Toni Pacini, who she says, "opened the door to the authors' world and then pushed me through it."

Saving Pvt. Limp Prick

Voices from the Dead 3

Paul Atreides

In his bedroom, watching him roll his service pistol over and over in his hands, I knew what he was thinking. He wanted to follow me. I wanted to shout at him to stop. He wouldn't have heard me. Hell, he couldn't see me, either. But I told him, anyway. In fact, I ordered him. Much like Lt. Dan ordered Forrest Gump in the movie, I barked my disapproval at Private First Class Limp Prick.

Limprey was his real name. I called him Limp Dick at times, too. He'd exhibited more bravery than any one of us while we tromped around villages luring out snipers and sniffing out bombs. As we passed a bottle of whiskey around one night in the rubble of a bombed and burned-out building, everyone told him how much they admired him for his courage. He insisted that wasn't the case; he wasn't brave at all. But we continued in our praise until, looking at the ground, he finally said, "If I really had as much courage as y'all say I do, I'd tell you I'm gay."

Our esteem rose higher, every one of us loved him more,

because of that one deed. *That* single admission took some mighty big balls. I affectionately started to call him Limp Wrist. He always laughed or gave me a shy smile. Yeah, Limp Wrist was one hell of a man.

But I didn't yell in any kind of friendly way when he hauled *me* out of the line of fire and saved my life. I hated him for it and called him a coward, told him it would've shown real courage to let me die.

One more week. *One more stinkin' week!* and I would've left there whole; as intact as God made me. The one my father preached about on Sunday mornings.

A hot fire-poker sting ripped through my flesh when the shrapnel hit. Blood splattered my right leg and the rivulets ran down the mangled remains of my left. I knew. I *knew*. When Limprey removed his hand from the shirt he'd packed into the wound between my legs and the expressions of the medics when they took over. I pleaded with them, begged them. Leave me alone. Let me go. They too ignored my pleas for mercy.

When I woke up in the med-tent, my leg and lower body bandaged and throbbing in pain, I cursed those motherfuckers. I cussed every one of them, from the nurse who administered the medication all the way down to Limp Dick. I let loose with a string of profanities I didn't even know I knew. I ripped the intravenous needles from my arms. When the second round of sedative wore off, I discovered my arms had been strapped down. I had to use my good leg. It hurt like a sonofabitch, but I managed to kick the IV pole far enough to yank the needles free again.

After that episode they laced me up as tight as a skate on

a hockey player. A couple days trussed up like a pork roast and I promised to behave myself if they would free my limbs.

Then they saved me from the medication I hoarded and swallowed to ease the pain in my head. That pain, the mental pain, was much worse than what wracked my body day and night. A pain so intense, there were times I couldn't even cry. Not one single goddam tear.

Then the good folks of the Army flew me back to the States and scheduled me to see one of their shrinks. I sat in that office for the allotted hour and every session went the same.

"I understand you didn't want to be saved. Why?"

"..."

"It says here in your chart," a flick of a finger against the file, "you repeatedly ripped your IVs out and had to be restrained. Why do you think you did that?"

"..."

"You hoarded pills and then swallowed a handful."

"..."

"Why did you want to die?"

I broke my silence, not with words but with action. I abruptly stood, undid my fatigue pants and dropped them to the floor.

The psychiatrist paused for a moment with a hand to her throat. She stood and my face clouded with anger when she dropped the file on the chair behind her. I wondered if she meant to grasp me in pity or to storm out of the room to report my insolence. Instead, she exposed her flat chest and the scars of a double mastectomy.

I laughed in anger and hurled the first words I'd spoken in all the weeks I'd been forced to see her. "That's a bullshit comparison. Look between your legs. At least you still have what makes you a woman," and walked out.

I faithfully attended the prescribed group therapy sessions and followed the same futile path.

"Sergeant Dennison, why don't you tell the group how you got here."

"..."

"Sergeant Dennison, share with the group how you feel about what happened."

"..."

"Sergeant Dennison, the men around you, many far more crippled than you, have expressed a will to live, but you haven't. Can you explain that to us?"

I looked around the room and saw plenty of missing feet or legs, missing hands, arms that ended in hooks, scarred chests, backs, and faces, missing ears and black patches covering empty eye sockets, but no evidence of a single injury to match my own.

"..."

It took a while, but I wised up, played their game, and they sent me home. My mom, God bless her, tried, though she had difficulty looking me in the eye without blushing over my injury. If any thoughts of gaining sympathy from my father entered my head, they were short-lived. The holier-than-thou bastard showed no mercy. "If the Almighty Lord had wanted you to be a father, he would've spared those things. It's His will; He knows best. Get on with life."

I tried. But, there's only one word to describe my

existence: torturous. Being anywhere in public reminded me I returned less than a man. Thanks to the local paper 'welcoming home the local hero,' people knew all about my injury. I should've sued, but what would that have accomplished? Nothing but continued humiliation. Did people think I didn't notice the piteous looks as I bagged their groceries, didn't feel the churning in my stomach at the attempts of condolence? Did they think I didn't notice the smirks? Or hear the snickers, the outright laughter, the derisive remarks? "There goes Sergeant Dickless." "Hey, look! It's Sergeant No-nuts!"

If I chanced to cross paths with a woman who caught my eye, like any man, my thoughts immediately were to approach her. In the next instant I'd chastise myself. How stupid! Who would want me? What woman wanted half a man? I didn't fool myself into thinking anyone would understand the sense of loss that invaded my every waking moment. Even the simplistic thing of seeing a man push his way through a restroom door and swagger up to a urinal, knowing I'd never be able to do that again, angered me beyond belief.

If days were horrendous, my nights were worse. I woke in a cold sweat from re-living attacks. Not of my own injuries, but of the body parts and blood raining down on us after an explosion – the aftermath of two of my men stepping on an IED; of a parade of dead eyes on the men I'd killed—enemies, yes, but men all the same—staring up at me in surprise and shock. Night after night, dreaming about making slow, sensuous love to some beautiful woman, explosive orgasms turned to utter devastation when I'd wake to the gaping cavity. Using tubes linked to bags instead of taking a piss like a man is no way to live. A man can face the loss or use of many different elements of his being. But to lose that, the one thing that named you male in the first place, and verifies you're a man, is indescribable agony. That scar of war was overwhelming and more than I could handle.

The nightmares never ended. I could think of no other way to put a stop to unbearable suffering. I drove to the nearest big city to an indoor firing range, paid the fees, went to the appointed lane, loaded a single bullet and pulled the trigger.

My parents didn't suffer over my death. They found solace in the church as they always had. When my brother died in a car accident shortly after he'd turned sixteen, my parents' grief was short; it was God's will and they wouldn't question it. Randall's photographs were put away and they never spoke his name again.

Do I have regrets? Only one: good old Private First Class Limp Prick. He came to visit me once at the hospital, to show me the medal he received for risking his life to save mine as bullets stung and impaled our bodies. I cursed him to his face, told him I couldn't hate him more; could not wish enough horrible things on his very existence.

I've watched him alone in his darkened room and heard his every whispered regret. "I'm sorry, but I couldn't let you go. I couldn't stand the thought of losing you." He expressed the guilt he feels for the burden I suffered. It so overwhelms his very soul, he's incapable of functioning. There could be no joy in his life, not even solitary pleasure; the river of the wound I inflicted ran that deep. Then I knew he felt my pain; fully understood it.

If I ever thought anyone would be able to imagine the depths of my injury. Shit… I should've known of all people, he'd be the one. He didn't perform that misdeed with intent of malice; he did so out of love for a fallen comrade. Probably more. I longed to reach out to embrace him, not only to offer solace and forgiveness, but to offer my apology.

I thought about a note I had stuffed into the pocket of his flak jacket. right after the first time our regiment took heavy fire. Five men in our company died. He tried to save them as he always did. They had been our friends, our comrades, our brothers.

Amid a brief lull in our deployment, I wrote, *Come on, Limp Prick, snap out of it! It's not your fault. Don't beat yourself up. You're the most courageous guy I've ever known. The bravest thing you can do right now, if you feel guilty for being alive when your brothers have died, is to forgive yourself and live to keep on fighting for them.*

He read it, thanked me, and stuffed it back into his pocket.

How could I stop him from following me?

Standing in his room, listening to his pleas of forgiveness, he couldn't hear or see me. I looked in his flak jacket hanging in his closet, finding the note right where he'd put it. Like a bookmark, I placed it into a novel on his nightstand, hoping he would see it, hoping I wasn't too late.

Paul Atreides is an award-winning playwright, author and theatre critic. A former critic and columnist with the Las Vegas Review-Journal, he now writes for EatMoreArtVegas.com. His work has also been featured in *Devoid*, a literary magazine of arts and culture.

His paranormal rom-com novels *Marvin's World of Deadheads, Jenna's Gang of Deadheads,* and *Nathan's Clan of Deadheads* make up the World of Deadheads trilogy (The Wild Rose Press).

The Last Confession won honors in three international script competitions. The 10-minute comedy *Tryst* won its category and placed third overall in Emerald Theatre's 6th Annual competition. His 10-minute drama *Fusion* is the finale piece of the *Grief Dialogues: In the Wake of Life* and has played around the country and in NYC.

www.paul-atreides.com

Facebook.com/paulatreides

The Basement of the World

Tom Coe

The boy moves forward slowly, listening to the echo of his tapping, the echo of his footsteps, the harshness of his breathing. Listening for something in the distance.

"Never go wandering through a door without a stick. Working light sources are rare. You could spend years in the dark, fumbling for switches, torches. Also, never light a candle or torch till you find a good anchoring spot. Listen up, boy, wasting matches, wasting batteries, all of that will get you killed; but being bind in the dark is a bad deal as well, so bring a stick, check the ground in front of you, find the holes and the rubble."

The wall leads to a corner where the boy's rod hits something. He kneels and picks it up. It is heavy, rounded and lumpy like a stone, but smoother, far smoother than any stone could be this far away from water to wear it down. It's cool to the touch. He makes a mental note, circle back, if possible, to investigate this object. He drops the stone back in its resting place.

Following a wall until the floor dips, he finds not a door but a nook. A small space where he discovers a table, but only after stumbling over one of its legs, then a set of chairs, four in all, circling the splintered wooden top. Running his hands across the surface, he finds an oil lamp, and holding it up, he can tell it's heavy. Sloshing sounds signal it contains fuel. Beside it lays a flint and a stone. These are rare, all in all, a momentous find. As he backs away, he stumbles over a squat metal canister filled with lamp oil. Amazing, but such a treasure should not be wasted or left behind. The tech of oil lamps is simpler than battery operated lights. Wicks can be improvised from scraps of cloth or paper, or if in true need, *flesh.*

The Instructor's words come out of the past, of the grisly things done to scrape by in the worst of times. "Never did it myself. Although I did resort to pulling out my hair, and Scrap-Paper, though weeping, volunteered some of his own papers. 'Better give up the written things that will let us live one more day,' he said. Always broke my heart to see him do it. Those pages were more than trinkets, more than little treasures to amuse himself. They were important. Every lil piece belonging to a greater whole. I'd do my best to track down extra paper for him to make up for the burning. To let him make copies.

"In time we found a small machine, some whirring thing with a needle at the end, with a glass jar attachment. It was a writing contraption. But a special one, it didn't write on paper. It wrote on skin. Scrap-Paper had read of such a machine, a 'tattoo gun' he called it, made to inscribe onto flesh, for what purpose he never said. 'It's possibly ritualistic. A way to make permanent designs for spiritual impact, but my purpose for it can best be called mundane,' he said. He took to marking his body with notes he viewed as important, critical enough to never be lost.

"In time we had him mark us with things we wanted to remember. Ink was hard to come by, and the ingredients were limited, so we volunteered our spit, our water, and in certain times, our blood to be mixed with ashes. When he was ready to die, he gave me his last request: My body is useless now. My flesh will tighten, break, and wither away. But I beg of you, preserve it, my friend, so I may continue to guide you.'

"When he passed, I did what we had all agreed to: upon death, we have the inked pieces of skin removed, flattened, stretched, and dried. Some of us had small patches. No more than a page worth, but he had covered his entire body in tightly packed text. By the time I collected all the notes, he was totally skinned. I wrapped his body in parchment to protect it. To preserve his writings, I sewed it together between two pieces of wood.

"This was his parting gift to us, the sum-total of his life's work. All the papers he wrote, all his notes of our times together, our names, our victories, our bitter losses, songs, stories. All of him preserved all of us. He is the link. He is the book, My Fallen Loved Ones."

That artifact now sits in front of the Boy, a collection of human leather, and paper pasted onto leather, a loosely organized cluster of knowledge. Next to schematics for the creation of unknown machines are the lyrics to a dirty limerick. Next to an advertisement for food neither the boy, nor the group before him ever ate, are accounts of marvelous runes etched on a black surface. Runes that flicker and dance before All the Practices for Living.

The Instructor had taken to reading aloud from the book to fill the emptiness, needing to hear his own voice in his isolation. When he discovered the boy, he began reading the book to him.

"At first, I wasn't sure what had happened to you. I suspected some form of crippling ailment made you small and feeble. But when I found a passage about the care of 'infants' which was noted by Scraps to relate to other writing about things called 'babies.' Wherever we come from, what is outside these halls, people come about from something called "birth." I am still trying to find out what that entailed, but it creates a new person, small, defenseless, needing to be cared for and taught things."

The boy never took to speaking, so the Instructor spoke to keep them company in the silence. The only sounds the boy made were grunts, cries, or coughs.

"One day, we'll have to find a name for you, Boy, one day you'll no longer be a boy."

THE BOY HACKS the legs off the table with a small ax he hangs from his bag, tying them together with rope he'd found in a nearby alcove. The area is littered with objects; he found containers of water and nails as well.

The Boy sets about repurposing the table. First severing the legs with a small saw, one of many tools hanging from his belt. He binds the legs together to be used for firewood later. With a small bit of chalk, he marks lines, the table to be cut smaller, the pieces lopped off and nailed to a frame to form walls. On one wall of the newly made box, he makes a hole with a hand-cranked drill, passing a rope through and tying it down. Inside he lays the lamp, the canister of oil, the rest of the rope and water.

"See, at a point, you'll grow, from baby to Boy. Then something else, maybe a man. Can't be calling you Man not really a name and doesn't ring as well as Boy."

The Boy pulls the box with the rope through the remainder of the room, the area longer than it is deep. The remaining alcoves hold little else, a few more tables and chairs. He manages to find matches and paper. The boy had been looking for something to practice writing on, the last thing The Instructor talked him through before going cold and stiff. He began teaching writing years before, as soon as the boy could hold a stick steady and stand on his own. Using his pointer finger to gesture towards a letter, intoning it as he moved over in the air to form its shape. The boy would repeatedly write letters and words in the sand as they went along, so as to not waste paper or flesh.

"You're too small and tender for the writing needle, but someday you'll be ready-"

The boy is wary of it, packed so far down inside his bag. To preserve the notes, he writes copies, although his letters are scratchy and lopsided.

"My hand was never as good as Scrap's," he hears in his head. "He had mastered it, a joy to look at, and a joy to watch him work." The room has been harvested, nothing else to take, nothing to come back for. The boy exits and pulls the hook from the wall, rewinding the large spool of red string before replacing it in his bag.

Hundreds of feet later, he enters a door, leading to a bigger area. Not a normal room, great echoes, rebounding off the sound of water in the distance. Could be an Anchor Point, "Never leave a hook in a door unless it got something worth coming back for, like fresh running water, or the dispensers."

The Boy carefully moves forward, counting steps. These are coveted finds, but the area is more dangerous than the layout of normal rooms. "Can't really call em' rooms, not sure what to call em'. All of them so big they echo, can't find the ceiling, the walls rarely straight. We don't go much further than where we found water. Sometimes we find edible things, but we've lost members to things that were poisonous, so we try to avoid those."

Tom Coe. Born of the tar, will return to the tar.

Raised under the oppressive heat of the desert sun, industrial wastelands, dying subdivisions, murder by neon.

Everyday drudgery hides horror, coiling around the throat, tentacles longer than the night, ghosts of regret and shame, ghouls of the dead freeways, sights and sounds to numb the senses, automatic disposal of your spent husk, I am ten seconds from your location. No one will believe what you saw.

A$$hole Dragon

H.G. McKinnis

Every time Drake turned around, he stumbled into his boss hovering over the frozen dragon, stroking the body, hands trembling.

"Ohmygod," Abe moaned. He stood, making a come-here motion. "Bring the forklifts down. We're ready to pull it out."

With every step into the glacier, the wet aroma of dirt under ice rose from Drake's feet. As the forks descended, their treads shook the remaining frost from the dragon. For a moment, he imagined the frozen skin expanding and contracting, knowing it was impossible. Then he shuddered. What if the machinery tore through the skin, or worse, broke off a limb? He raised his hand to stop the drivers, "Hold up," he yelled, "Let's take this slow."

The custom-built forks slowly moved their slim, flexible tines under the edge of the animal, lifting it by increments. Blades squeezed under as the crew braced the body. Gloves padded against the elements slid shims beneath the corpse, then waited for the forks to edge forward. Finally, the crew maneuvered a canvas beneath their prize.

Sweat froze Drake's goggles to his face. He smelled the tension in his team. They exuded fear; fear of failure, of catastrophe, and of a no-bonus paycheck. They needed to pull the dragon out immediately. Wait too long and the ice would solidify, wasting all their work, leaving the dragon cemented back in place.

Drake found himself praying they could lift the animal out in one piece. "Dr. Goldman?" he asked over the com, using Abe's title. "Can we move the dragon?"

No answer.

Toes almost over the edge of the pit, dark rimmed eyes fixed on the corpse, Abe stood. Below him, ankle deep in slush the crew waited.

"Abe!" Drake yelled. "We have to move it, now!"

As if awakened from a dream, the man started. "Right," he said, "Do it!" He raised his hands, and the forks swiveled to pull the canvas taut, lifting the body from the icy muck. They drove to a pallet and laid the corpse with exquisite delicacy into the foam-covered case, custom made in a Chinese factory.

As the crew adjusted the desiccated dragon inside, Drake realized his job was over. His steps slowed as he followed the forklifts. A cargo plane squatted at the end of the ramp; the nose cone tilted in a yawn. The lifts rumbled into the dark interior, a belly-of-the-beast vibe coming from within. At the back of the plane the forks lowered the case onto the deck, and staring until the last possible moment, Drake dodged as the drivers backed out.

Moving from the darkness, he made his way to the Quonset huts where his people worked to seal up the labs and pack away the equipment. For one insane moment, Drake thought about running into the pit and signing his name on an electrical generator, or melter, hell, anything that would let the world know, that he, Drake Rossi, had been part of the team to unearth the dragon.

Abe's labored steps sounded behind him. "Drake, you've been integral in coordinating the crews for the disinterment, and I need someone to get the labs at Helsinki reconfigured. Would you be interested in coming to work at the university?"

Drake knew that hopping up and down squealing with joy might damage his manly reputation. He nodded with what he hoped looked like gravitas. *Act cool,* he told himself. "What would the job entail?" his voice squeaked. He coughed to cover his excitement.

"Your position comes with an increase in pay, and a yearly contract."

I'm staying with the dragon. The words sing-song-ed in his head, leaving him feeling like a kid with his first video game.

A shift in temperature sharpened his gaze, and the interior of the plane darkened as the crew pulled the loading straps tight around the crate. The hair on the back of Drake's neck stood up. This might be the last flight he ever took.

Knock it off, he told himself. Why he would have a suicidal longing on the best day of his life, he had no idea. But Death fluttered around, a dark butterfly teasing with promise.

Low blood sugar messing with his head, no doubt. His stomach growled in agreement. He could use a break from the dark thoughts which had plagued him all his life, now manifesting in this oppressive dimness.

Abe waited patiently for his answer.

"An intriguing offer," Drake said. Intriguing. Hell, six weeks ago his plans centered on not waking up in the morning. The dragon's existence mixed mythology with science. If he'd known dragons were real, he'd have spent his college years studying the crap out of them. "I'll give Helsinki a try."

INSIDE THE PLANE, carpenters installed seats as electricians powered up the heaters attached to them. Drake waited for the heat to kick on, while Abe talked on and on about the benefits of the new job. Already sold, Drake nodded at required intervals and tuned out the words. When his boss reached a stopping point, Drake raced to his car. He fished out his backpack. The second he closed the door, he realized someone would have to drive the beat-up Horizon into Helsinki. He sent a text to an electrician on his crew. 'Wanna make some extra cash?'

The man sent a thumbs up with a party horn.

Leaving the keys under the floor mat, Drake sprinted onto the plane. After he stowed his belongings, he stood in front of the dragon's crate. The crew continued filling the plane's cavernous hold with equipment and supplies, but the space around their prize remained empty, a sacrosanct area. Nothing was allowed close to Abe's remarkable find.

Drake dropped into the seat next to Sam, the project manager. "Can I ask a question?"

The older man glanced up from his phone, "Sure."

"The minute I walked up to the table, you put me in charge

of the electricians. You didn't know anything about me. What if I'd fucked up the install?"

"What if *you'd* fucked up?" Sam laughed. "Randal and Tomas both bombed. Before you arrived, I'd been overseeing the electricians as well as doing my own job. You worked out." He put a beer can to his lips and tipped it back. "You were the only guy who showed up with European equipment. When you told me that, I almost kissed you." He laughed again. "You were this project manager's dream come true."

Drake felt the fast-track rolling under him, Team Helsinki all the way. Something would go wrong, it always did, but until they threw him out, he would stick with the dragon as they unraveled the mystery of its existence.

The plane rumbled over the gravel, bumping and jostling until liftoff. The flight put them all in high spirits. They drank, sang, and joked. When a two-note chime played over and over sounding like a child's toy xylophone, they ignored it.

Abe jumped up. "The dragon!" he yelled.

"The dragon!" Everyone cheered, lifting their drinks in salute.

Drake realized the chiming was the crate's alarm. He struggled out of his seat to head into the hold.

"Look," Abe pointed to a blinking red light.

Great, the monitoring system was offline. Drake needed to fix that before they landed, otherwise Abe would have to do a ton more paperwork.

"Can you get it working?" Abe's face glistened with sweat. They both knew his reputation hinged on getting the dragon to the university intact. Helsinki's Cryptozoology department would be the world's foremost experts on dragons, but only if Abe came back with a properly certified body.

Drake pulled out his multimeter and clipped it to the cord of the generator. He checked the voltage and the battery. Dead. He moved the meter to the TEMCo Euro-Plus Transformer TT1003 - 15 kVA. *Shit,* he'd rigged it to go from European voltage to US no wonder it wasn't working, he flipped the switch to take power directly from the plane, which ran on US standard. So much for his job offer.

Abe must have seen something in his expression, "You can fix it, right?"

"Just did," Drake said. He ran a hand over his beard. "I forgot the plane used American power.

The color faded from Abe's face, and Drake wondered if the guy would pass out. "Don't worry." Drake patted the dragon's container. "The sensors haven't gone critical. It'll be fine when we land."

"We have to bring this back perfectly intact." Abe's eyes went wild. "You have no idea what is riding on this animal."

Drake knew his job hung in the balance. He needed to get Abe's hysteria under control. "We got it on board in pristine condition. It will be fine when we unload. But even if it is a bit smudged, Jesus H. Christ, Abe. It's a fucking dragon."

Abe's shoulders straightened as he laid a hand on the case. "This is real," he said. "It *is* a fucking dragon." He stood up and pulled his cell. "I'll make some calls and schedule one of the university trucks to meet us at the airport." He started back to his seat, punching numbers on his phone.

The man definitely needed a wrangler. Drake let hope creep back in.

Half an hour later, Abe, all smiles, held up his cell to show a news feed. The excavation site filled the screen. Drake saw his parking space filled with snow. Then Helsinki-Vantaa International airport appeared as a seething mass of people. Cars backed up on the freeways for miles in all directions. Their dragon wasn't just news; it was *THE* news.

The pilot came on the intercom, "Due to increase of traffic at Helsinki-Vantaa we land at Turku."

"Turku!" Randal yelled, in his usual mania. "Turku's in the middle of nowhere!" Why the man kept his job, Drake never understood and he winced as Randal rattled the handle of the cockpit's door. When that didn't work, he pounded on it. The pilot ignored him. "I need to be on camera," Randal bellowed. The loss of his forthcoming stardom filled the windowless fuselage with anguished cries.

Drake felt darkness close in, the cabin entombing him in a windowless prison. Great, he'd acquired a brand-new case of claustrophobia. Normally, he sought the comforting embrace of small spaces, but thoughts, alien and raw, echoed through his mind. He took a deep breath and let it out slowly. In . . . two, three, four, and out . . . two, three. His heart slowed, beating a calmer rhythm. Hands flexed and stretched, the fingers splaying out, imaginary talons growing from the tips. He closed his eyes and leaned his seat back, breathing. In, two, three, four…

Rhythmic banging from the hold combined with bucking from the plane woke him. He tightened his seatbelt, wondering why the pilot hadn't announced—

"Mayday, mayday, mayday," the pilot yelled over the intercom. In a quieter voice he added, "We're going down."

That sounded bad. Drake elbowed Sam. "What do we

do?"

Sam shoved a bag of chips under his seat and bent down as if to smell his knees. "Brace for impact." His fingers interlocked above his head.

Emotions detached, Drake watched the crew as if from the cargo area. Folded sacks of meat, he thought, and his stomach rumbled with hunger.

An explosion from behind, and Drake jerked his head. The dragon's crate lay in pieces. Shit. No dragon, no job and no—

A huge grey head appeared, mouth open to display rows of obsidian teeth the size and shape of ancient scythes. The animal seemed to smile as it stalked toward the passengers. The plane rocking under the dragon's shifting weight, fell into a dive. Eyes wide, the beast slid forward, scrabbling for purchase, managing to wedge a claw under Drake's seat.

In reflex, Drake picked up his feet, crouching in fetal position. The huff from the huge animal's breath wafting up from the floor added to his terror.

The plane banked, throwing the beast sideways into the bulkhead. Without losing focus, the dragon slid its head under Drake.

The plane dove forward, slamming the animal into the seat again. "Almost down," the pilot yelled over the intercom.

Fucking fabulous. Drake's hands fumbled undoing the seatbelt. He refused to be on the menu. Too close to his arm, the dragon's claws began ripping away at the plane's frame, puncturing the housing.

As the air streamed in, it mixed with hysterical screaming followed by stampeding feet.

Trading a quick meal for a quick exit, the dragon worked

its diamantine claws into the new hole, ignoring the plane's shudders as it bounced down the runway. Pushing itself out, it fell onto the asphalt in a hail of gear boxes, splinters, and foam.

The pilot wrestled the screeching plane to a jostling halt far from a connecting gate sleeve.

Drake had to tell Abe. He rolled out of his seat. "The dragon—"

Abe nodded. "I saw."

Sirens wailed, the pitch lowering as the vehicles neared. Giving Abe a hand up, Drake made his way to the hole in the side of the plane. The dragon lay on the runway, sides heaving.

Randal moved alongside, his camo rifle in hand. Where, Drake wondered, had he stashed that thing?

Sighting down the barrel, Randal took his shot. A round slammed into the ground next to the dragon. "Don't worry, I've got this," he slurred. His next shot blew a hinge off the crumpled dragon crate, and the beast rose with a snarl to head toward the plane. A limp slowed it down.

Flinching back, Randal slurred. "You'd think that thing was immune to bear tranq." He grabbed shells from his pocket. "These should work."

Abe intercepted his hand, "Let Drake handle this. He's not drunk off his ass."

"It's my gun, and my ammo." Randal's teary voice continued. "My gun. My ammo." He waved toward the limping dragon. "I brought the armament."

Drake grabbed the gun, fumbling to chamber the shells. His hand shook. "Odd," he thought, "I don't feel nervous."

Putting the stock to his shoulder, he pulled the trigger. Stunned when the shot went directly into a grey-scaled hip.

The dragon's lumpy head turned toward him. Lifting one brow as if in inquiry, it collapsed on the tarmac, a lifeless heap.

"Oh shit," a voice said, and Drake realized it was his own.

Abe motioned the crew out. "Go, go!"

Cradling the gun in numb arms Drake almost tripped as he ran down the ramp. He slowed as he neared the prostrate body, stopping to place one trembling hand against leathery scales. "Impossible," he thought, and yet the dragon breathed.

H. G. McKinnis works nights on the Las Vegas strip helping gear up the dragon army at the Tournament of Kings show. By day she crafts stories about a hopeful, yet headstrong dragon trying to survive and perhaps thrive in the hardscrabble world of science and mythology. *A$$hole Dragon* is currently in the final edits. Her novel *A Justified Bitch*, published by Imbrifex, is available for those who want to read about quirky off-strip Las Vegas.

They Call It Girl

Leah Marks

They called it a girl. It wasn't sure what a "girl" was, but that was how they referred to it.

Looking at itself in the dim reflection of a shiny surface mounted on the wall, it saw a roundish shape featuring an arrangement of holes and bumps in front and dark coils and wisps draping from the top. It opened its mouth and watched in the reflection as a ringed hollow appeared. A wet pink worm wriggled within. Weird. It furrowed its brow and squinted, attempting to make the reflection shift but couldn't see clearly with its eyes narrowed to slits.

Stupid.

Detecting motion in its periphery, it turned to see two figures in white enter the room from an unknown opening in the wall that appeared and then disappeared. It turned back to the panel on the wall and scrunched its nose and mouth into different shapes, watching the reflected changes.

"What's she doing?" the shorter one asked in a sharp voice.

"I believe this is the first time she has seen her own reflection," the tall one said.

"She hasn't spoken yet?"

"Sounds. Not words." Tall One turned their head from side to side. It mimicked their movements, though it wasn't sure why.

"She understands us?"

Tall One ignored the question and stepped closer to it, lifting their hand in greeting. It lifted its own hand in response and then looked at the appendage curiously. Very similar. Was Tall One a girl, too? They had the same front features, though their face shape was more square than round, and the coils on top were lighter and shorter. Tall One's body had a big middle, and their vocalizations were lower. Did those differences matter? What was a girl? It hadn't figured that out yet. Confused, it turned to look at the people in white.

Waiting.

Tall One reached out with their hand. For what purpose, it didn't know.

"No direct contact until the nanoalignment analysis confirms she's stabilized." A voice crackled from above. The sound startled it. Looking around the room, it tried to find the source of the bodiless voice.

Above them was a single large plane of softly glowing light that brightened and dimmed in a slow pulse and emitted a static hum. This was called a ceiling, they told it. It did not know why ceilings hummed, but it liked the sound. Still searching for the source of the voice, it began to hum along, trying to match the frequency. There wasn't a body on the ceiling where the voice must have come from. Nothing there but light. The only flaw on the perfect glowing surface was a black box in the corner. It studied the box to see if a person could come from there. It didn't think so. A body would not be able to fit in that box.

The pulsing light faded before a column of brighter light shone down upon where it stood. The light showed things that had not been there before. Small dots in the air drifted upward, barely visible. It lifted its hand to catch them, but found nothing there.

Strange.

"Results are in. Neural response is still nonlinear," the noncorporeal voice said. This time it was able to discern where the voice had come from. There *was* a person in the box!

"Has she demonstrated mastery of the behavioral requirements, at least?" the sharp-voiced person asked.

"Does that matter?" Tall One folded their arms across their chest. It looked down at its own arms and crossed them across its torso, trying to match the configuration. Not the same. "Have you ever seen the Registrar-Adjunct ignore abnormalities? Anomalies are always slated for termination."

"Another series of behavioral tests, then, to prove viability." the box voice said.

Tests. It recognized the word. A series of activities that, if done correctly, would result in treats. It loved the treats. Lived for them. It dropped its arms and looked at the two figures in pleased expectation.

Another person in white arrived, carrying an armful of green lengths, each tipped with colorful and unusually shaped segments sprouting from the center. These were called flowers; it had been told. The person placed them atop the flat raised surface where it usually consumed its meals. There were many words to remember. Words for everything. Some were simple, so it could pick them out easily in the room. Ceiling. Floor. Table. Chair. Other words were more difficult to understand. Girl.

The first time it saw flowers, they had been placed on the table where it ate. So it had stuffed several into its mouth. Horrible. It soon learned what flowers were for. Not eating. They were to be positioned in a tall, clear container so that no one color or shape overwhelmed any other until the grouping produced approval from the observers in the room. This was a simple test of a skill a girl should have. For what reason, it did not know. Flowers did nothing, even once positioned correctly. They didn't even taste good.

It got to work inspecting each flower for discoloration or tears before stripping the lower half of the lengths and setting them in the container. Then, it rotated and repositioned them until it deemed the task was done. It looked at the observers in the room and waited to be told it had done well and to receive its treat.

Tall One examined the arrangement and then patted it on its head.

"Good girl."

It held out its hand, expecting the reward, but received nothing.

"Let's move on to the next test."

It sighed, but there was nothing to be done. There would be a treat after the next test. It followed the two figures through a different opening, one that also appeared and disappeared, and into another space. Random items were strewn haphazardly on the floor and across tables and chairs and other larger objects positioned around the room. An organizational task. Harder, but certainly manageable. A test of memory and placement.

It collected the scattered items and relocated them to their designated places. It went through the motions, not caring for the act itself, but eager to enjoy the treats that would come after.

Once all the items had been put away, it collected the instruments used for an activity called cleaning. Another important skill. First, it rubbed a small piece of fabric sprayed with liquid that was not for drinking along the surfaces of the objects in the room. Then, it maneuvered a tall device to the center, pulling a long black line from its belly and connecting it to holes in the wall. Holes not for touching. Pressing a button activated a sudden spike of discordant sound. It pushed the noisy device along the floor, each pass leaving a clean stripe.

Once finished, it put the cleaning instruments back in their enclosures, ready for the observers to complete an inspection. It waited to be told it had done well and to receive the overdue treat.

"Good job, girl."

It held out its hand, expecting two treats to be dropped into it. But again received nothing. The small but essential ritual that usually followed its tests never happened.

It frowned.

No treat? But it had completed both activities successfully. Its mind circled the point repeatedly, its body tense. This was not the way tests were supposed to go. It didn't understand what was happening.

"Next test," the box voice said.

Another being walked in through the opening, not in white, and it knew what was next. The test it liked least of all. The figure disrobed, exposing a part that it did not have on its own body: a column of flesh below their belly that protruded outward.

"Is this necessary? She's already performed adequately and has successfully completed this type of testing before." The sharp-voiced person spoke to the box.

"She must pass an assimilative evaluation before introduction to the population."

Tall One gestured to the other side of the room toward a large, raised platform.

But what about the treat?

Reluctantly, it obeyed, moving to sit on the squishy surface where this test was always performed. It laid back.

The person approached and climbed onto the platform as well, laying their body atop it, a round and foreign landscape pressing down heavily. Their hands stroked down its body, alternately squeezing and soothing. Their mouth locked onto its. No invasion of a wet pink worm this time, though. Nice.

IT ENDURED THE FEELING of being trapped, surrounded until it seemed like air was scarce and it was in a sweaty vacuum of compression and hot breath. The initial insertion always caught and dragged, but after a brief sting they slid through without resistance. It wasn't long before the being increased the speed and force of their movements, and the resulting punching of its core radiated a razor-edged pain that flared through to its back.

It made the sounds it knew it was supposed to make to get the treat it wanted. Hums and 'oohs' at intervals that were synced with the motion of their rocking bodies, faster and harder, increasingly violent, increasingly erratic, until the end. Finally, the person collapsed on top of it, damp and warm and heaving. It hated this part the most. What seemed an endless moment later, it was freed from its prison as the other person got up, patted its head, and left the room.

It sat up. Waited. Hand outstretched for its treat. But the two observers stood still, making no move to put their hands in their white draping where the treats were usually stored.

"Behavioral output is contextually accurate despite low neural engagement," the box voice said.

"Do you think that's enough for her to be released?"

There were no treats in sight. No treat. No treat. No treat. But there was always a treat. That was the way things worked. Expected behavior produced treats. Its compliance in return for reward.

Breath shortened. Muscles tensed. Vision narrowed.

"There's progress, but no. She may mimic behavioral assimilation, but that's learned and not innate. Better than nothing but not good enough to graduate the program," the box voice said.

Its chest tightened as if the space inside it were shrinking. The room, usually cool and comfortable, turned warm.

"Plus, she lacks the functional communicative ability

necessary to adapt successfully," Tall One added. "Further instruction will be required. And more tests."

Each attempt to inhale was difficult. Inside something broke, and what had been contained fractured into chaos.

Voices rose, but it did not listen. Every correction it had absorbed, every softened edge, every instruction exploded at once. Objects flew across the room and broke apart. Fabric shredded. Hands that grabbed it were twisted and torn. Flowers heaved and glass shattered. A body struck the floor and did not move again. White became stained with red.

A new figure rushed into the room, and it saw what was in their hands. Just as abruptly as it had started, it stopped. It stood among the damage, breath heaving but eyes locked on the newcomer, one hand opened, ready for the treat it deserved.

The figure edged forward and dropped their offering into its hand before slowly backing away. It looked down at its prize. The pressure that usually sat in its chest was gone, replaced by a clean and hollow quiet. For the first time in a long time, there was nothing twisting inside. It looked down at the motionless body at its feet and then once more at the treat in its hand.

They called it a girl. It let them. It retreated to a corner, holding the treat half forgotten in its hand as it surveyed the destroyed room and felt relief.

Leah Marks has called Las Vegas home since 2019, though in truth she lives wherever her characters are. When she can step away from her marketing operations career, she reads, travels, and chases new adventures, especially ones she hasn't tried yet. Polyamorous and LGBTQ, she is drawn to connection in all its shifting forms. Skill-building is less a hobby than a compulsion: her craft room overflows with strange tools, half-learned arts, and glorious experiments in progress, much to the chagrin of her partners, Duke and Kit. She is always learning, always moving toward the unknown, and always ready for the next story.

The Bannerman

Diana Fedorak

Metal prongs clang into my shoulder harness. The claw is in command now. It swings me through the cargo bay of my lord's ship. Green numbers flash in my helmet visor, displaying my azimuth and altitude. My thrust vector boots are powered on. Flexing my gloves, I activate my gesture-based haptic controls. The hatch to *LMS Lodi* opens wide.

Below, the azure curve of planet Manius glistens. In the distance, the other eminent houses have arrived. The largest craft, the emperor's, has already positioned its giant optical array. The sensor sparkles, ready to catch the laser of the first bannerman who reaches it. "House Lodi. Launch in T minus sixty seconds," says the officer from the emperor's corps. Quickly, I count three other ships, doors open, ready to deploy their bannermen.

My ship's name reflects my sovereign, ruler of planet Azeria, conqueror of the scarpland and fire, and lord to our house, who was assassinated, most likely by House Valero. Taking a deep breath, I whisper a prayer. "Gods, grant me my destiny as Seraphina, daughter of Lodi, and his sole heir. I ask for your strength to declare Manius in my father's name."

Manius, the planet of nectar and crystal indri beckons. Whoever rules it shall control the galaxy's supply of healing forevermore. Instead of designating its ruler as my mother, as is the custom, in the aftermath of my father's treacherous death, the emperor has pitted us against one another in a bannermen's race. "Cunning," my mother said of our ruler. "And dangerous. Whoever rules Manius will likely marry his heir."

As if I give a damn about being mated to the Crown Prince. I rather like my freedom. Plus, I'm more interested in rumors of Lord Valero's condition. When I claim Manius, I will deny him healing. Let him suffer an agonizing death.

"T-minus thirty seconds." I focus on the green continent below. Stowed on my back is my banner kit, complete with a laser beacon. The other houses won't outrun fire. I've bested all of them in training. The lone exception is Lucian Valero, son of Lord Valero. In our youth, we often tied.

Gears spin in the claw as it angles me headfirst toward Manius. "T-minus ten." I inhale and tuck in my arms. My toes are pointed, and my visor displays the ready logo. "Launch."

The release jerks me a few degrees off course, and I fire my thrusters immediately. The diamond in my visor bounces, and it takes me a good thirty seconds to align it with the intended flight path. I initiate maximum velocity.

A yellow streak on my right keeps pace alongside me. Lucian Valero, no doubt. Clenching my fists, I concentrate on my readings.

The continent looms ahead. To my left fly House

Ballantine and House Lewin, based on their black and ruby exosuits. My calculations show I'm ahead of them by nearly a minute. The blinking red temperature indicates I'm entering Manius's atmosphere. I keep my chin down so my shoulder nozzles stream the plasma shield over my body, which fully envelops me.

My attitude indicator holds steady. The roar of the mesosphere's heat rages against my plasma shield. I'm golden if I can keep this flight profile steady.

BAM!

The green landform swings wildly out of my visor's field-of-view. I'm tumbling, splayed ass over back. Alarms crescendo. What the hell?!

Something strikes me. I throw my hands out front and cinch my legs together to stabilize my heading. I'm wildly off course. Gasping, I fight the slipstream to bring my arms in. No use—I'm too fast. A yellow exosuit shoots ahead of me. A blast of blue light zips in my direction, barely missing my pack.

Valero, that dick! Weapons were strictly forbidden in the race of bannermen, but he likely disguised his blaster as the banner's laser in his pack. He must have clipped me. And to think, I obeyed the rules when the emperor's officer inspected me.

"Hear me, Gods, I will reach Manius before Lucien Valero even if it means I draw my last breath." I ease back on my throttle a tad, just enough to bring my arms to my chest. Now! I slam them back against my thighs. Full speed—check! Plasma shield—functional! As for the small circle with the yellow exosuit bouncing around in it, I'm gaining on him.

Another ray whizzes by my helmet. C'mon! But this attack cost him speed, as Valero had to slow to fire once he no longer needed his plasma shield. Grinding my jaw, I steepen my angle-of-attack downward.

My shield shuts off. I'm fully in the troposphere, baby! Clouds whoosh by. My visor shows that I'm still ahead of Ballantine and Lewin. Two more minutes until touch down.

Stay on course, stay on course. There! I've overtaken Valero. Passing his circle in my visor, I give him a wink. I'll have to find a way to disarm him after I land. The ground is rushing up at me. We all chose a grassy plain, with no weapon in sight. All I have is my banner's mast, the pointy end.

CLANK! My arms flay around. What the—my jump pad somersaults away from my body. It must have loosened from my pack when that bastard tagged me. I pull the ripcord to my chute.

The streamers yank me up, a few thousand feet above ground. Damn Valero. His jump pad inflates fully. He slows his reverse thrusters above it. Given my rate of descent in the chute, he'll have his banner raised before I hit the ground. I have only one shot at this.

My hand reaches up, and I yank down on the release. I plunge toward his pad, cutting off power completely. I keep my knees bent and folded together, otherwise I'm liable to bounce a mile away.

Valero touches land. I thump onto his pad. Springing high, I throw my body in the opposite direction. My midsection crashes into Valero's helmet. I slam into the ground. Am I dead…or am I paralyzed? Either way, I can't breathe. After a moment, I unlatch my helmet. Fresh, grassy-scented air imbues my lungs with hope.

With a grunt, I raise myself on an elbow. Valero staggers up. I reach for my pack and find my mast. Pointy end—I drive it in his spine. He crumples. I plant the stake into the ground and strain to rise on my wobbly legs. While he moans, I kick him in the ribs. He curls up like a caterpillar.

I yank free my banner. Unfurling it, I clip it onto the mast. Now for the beacon. As I steady its tripod, Valero seizes my ankle. Tripping, I knock over my beacon. He crawls for his blaster in the long grass. I flick my wrist, and my thrusters shoot me up. Another flick, and my boot crashes down on his hand wrapped around his weapon. He shouts, and I wrestle the blaster away from him.

"Take off your helmet!"

On his knees, he complies and raises his hands. His sapphire-blue eyes meet mine in a sulk. I'm reminded of our youth when our mothers tried to match us. Until I rebelled.

"Tell me the truth. Did you kill my father?" I aim the blaster at his heart.

"No." He shakes his head.

"Don't lie to me!" I really should kill him.

"It was my stepsister, Yelene, on my stepmother's orders. My father knows nothing of it." His chest heaves, and weariness overcomes his otherwise noble bearing.

"Then why did you shoot me?"

"Because my father is ill, and I knew you would deny him healing because of what Yelene has wrought. If you must exact retribution, take my life instead. But please, help my father." His shoulders slump.

Hmmm. Well this is a conundrum. My prior rebellion

against my mother's wishes succeeded because she was wary of the new Lady Valero at the time.

"I'll grant your wish to spare your father, but you owe me." I press the trigger. He screams and clutches his upper arm. "Stay there," I command.

On the far side of the meadow, House Ballantine bounces on his pad. Not far, House Lewin's pad inflates.

I rush for the beacon and erect it. The laser rod slides into place, and I lock it, aimed at the sky. All green lights on the control console. From my pack, I slide on googles.

"Close your eyes," I say to Valero.

He obeys.

I press the fire button.

Above, my banner ripples in the breeze. A ring of orange flames, the sigil of House of Lodi.

Yelene, I'm coming for you.

Diana Fedorak is a speculative fiction writer from Las Vegas, Nevada. Born in Saigon, South Vietnam, she grew up in a Pan Am family who frequently traveled overseas. In a prior life, she served as a Colonel in the United States Air Force. She enjoys writing complex characters in high-stakes science fiction and fantasy worlds.

Diana's debut novel, Children of Alpheios, was released by The Wild Rose Press in early 2023 and won numerous awards. When she's not writing, she spends time in her own universe with her husband, two children, and their German Shepard.

ACKNOWLEDGMENTS

The SCWG anniversary anthology has been the most gratifying project for Blueberry Lane Books yet. As it celebrates a collaborative effort involving a certain amount of cross-editing of stories, thanks largely go to all the attending critique members on behalf of the active writing members inspired by our founder Toni K. Pacini.

Thank you to Skinny Dugans and your wonderful staff for ten years of hospitality.

Special thanks to author Lucy Couch (who happens to appear on the cover with her husband Ian Sweet Couch) and EJ Siegler who agreed to the critical task of last stage proofreading.

And as always, the great support work of Chris Falchetti whose team first sifted through the stories.

Apologies to anyone I might have missed in the finishing flurry.

ABOUT THE EDITORS

BEN PARRIS, best known for his Kindle bestseller *Wade of Aquitaine*, and for *Creds: The IRS Adventure*, is an author, editor, and educator.

He has published numerous short stories, completed eight books, edited at least twenty-one, and consulted on many more. His previous anthologies include *Drastic Measures*, *Wash the Spider Out*, and *Universal Enigma*. Outside of literary pursuits, he enjoys studying history, hiking, and playing chess. Join his Facebook fan page at:

www.facebook.com/BenParrisAuthor.

H.G. MCKINNIS can neither spell nor punctuate, but can wrangle words and phrases. Having honed her editing expertise in the wild, she has practiced on her feral writer friends. Every so often this ability comes in handy, thus this editing project. This is her first anthology.

https://imbrifex.com/book/a-justified-bitch/

www.ingramcontent.com/pod-product-compliance
Lightning Source LLC
LaVergne TN
LVHW091051080826
845145LV00002B/711

* 9 7 8 1 9 4 2 1 8 3 2 1 1 *